M000084294

EXPOSING ELE

By: Rebecca Gober & Courtney Nuckels

Clean Teen Publishing

THIS book is a work of fiction. Names, characters, places and incidents are the product of the authors' imagination or are used factiously. Any resemblance to actual persons, living or dead, business establishments, events or locales is entirely coincidental.

NO part of this book may be reproduced, scanned, or distributed in any printed or electronic form without permission. Please do not participate in or encourage piracy of copyrighted materials in violation of the author's rights. Purchase only authorized editions.

EXPOSING ELE

Copyright ©2012 Rebecca Gober & Courtney Nuckels

CLEAN TEEN PUBLISHING

Cover Design by: Marya Heiman
Typography by: Courtney Nuckels
Editing by: Cynthia Shepp

Content Disclosure

For more information about our content disclosure, please
utilize the QR code above with your
smart phone or visit us at

www.cleanteenpublishing.com.

ONE

Chaos abounds all around us.

Tony, my protector, stands before me in a defensive stance while Zack's sinister glare penetrates me to the core. To say that Zack and I don't get along is a bit of an understatement. He and his dad tried to turn me into a lab experiment after they attempted to kill my friends.

I shiver at the sight of his bizarrely formed eyes and I grip Lily, Connor's little sister, a bit tighter to my chest in response. Thankfully, she's still passed out and is completely unaware of the danger we are in.

For a few seconds no one moves or breathes; we just wait and watch to see if the other will make the first move. Even though I desperately want to, I don't dare break away from Zack's gaze. I watch in horror as the colors continue to swirl through half of his iris, while the outer half turns a crimson, blood red. He grins eerily and Tony raises his gun a little higher.

Suddenly a sound like a freight train breaks our staring match. We all turn in unison to watch a multitude of helicopters begin surrounding the area. Large black SUVs pull up around us on all sides, entrapping us like

1

circus animals. I find myself stunned, in awe at the sight of working vehicles. It seems like forever since I've seen any type of running automotive, much less an aircraft.

Not wasting any time gawking, Tony yanks my hand and rushes Lily and me into the nearby brush while Zack is distracted. I watch as Zack turns around quickly and realizes we are gone. He looks royally pissed, but he starts moving in the direction of the SUV's.

The brush that we are hiding in is still a few hundred yards from the tree line and, truth be told, I don't think we could make it without someone spotting us for sure. Some of the others we've rescued, around fifteen in all, huddle around us, trying desperately to hide as well. We all try our best to find cover between the wispy blades of grass, but it seems futile.

Something bad is about to happen, I can feel it in my bones. The brush offers us little protection and I know that if I don't turn us invisible, and soon, our chances of being seen increase tenfold. I've never tried to mask this many people before, but I have no choice but to try. I look around and, unfortunately, I don't see any other purple eyes amongst us. Realizing that it's up to me, I have everyone that is with us place one of their hands on me. Tony holds my left hand and I hold Lily tight with my right arm. The poor thing still hasn't woken up, but that's probably best right about now. Tony links his fingers between mine. I don't have time to process how intimately he's holding my hand, so I concentrate on turning us invisible.

"Did it work?" I ask Tony, since I can still see us

even if we are invisible. It's one of my other gifts.

He looks down at our hands and whispers, "Yes."

I fight back the feeling that I am being drained of power and energy, focusing instead on what is happening just twenty yards in front of us. The helicopters are hovering over the clearing and the trucks sit idle, apparently waiting for instruction. The masses of people are still one big blur of confusion.

I spot Zack and his father, Dr. Hastings, standing off to the side next to one of the SUVs. Dr. Hastings holds what looks to be some sort of remote control in his hand. Zack is holding his right hand high up in the air, watching for what looks to be a particular moment to release it. As soon as his arm comes down, all of the helicopters open up and ropes fall fluidly to the ground. Men in black uniforms begin rappelling out of the helicopters, making their way down to solid ground. Simultaneously, the SUV doors begin opening and swarms of men in the same black uniforms begin piling out of the vehicles, armed with automatic weapons.

I watch as Dr. Hastings pulls an antenna out of the remote control device and presses several buttons. At the same time, Zack pulls out a large pair of headphones and places them over his ears. Within a few seconds, to my dismay, all of the Reapers that had been fighting up until this point begin dropping to the ground, cupping their ears as a high pitch noise reverberates around the mountainside.

I must have cringed a bit because Tony instantly becomes worried. "Willow, what's wrong?"

With my hands full, I attempt to rub my ear against my shoulder, trying to get the sound to stop. "It's the noise," I tell him. "It's hurting my ears."

He looks at me in confusion. "What noise?"

I furrow my brow, trying to understand why I hear the noise and he doesn't. I look back out to the field and note that, indeed, only the Reapers are affected by the noise. Dr. Hastings's remote device must be omitting a sound that only a Reaper could hear. That has to be why Zack is sporting the headphones.

Everyone else has stopped fighting each other. They stumble about, confused, as the army of men circle in on them.

It only takes a few seconds for the peacefulness to reinstate itself back into chaos. The people that are in the clearing begin running away from the men holding the large ammunition guns. The 'soldiers' are indistinguishable, with black fabric covering every square inch of their body. The only thing you can see is their eyes that peer through small slits made in their masks.

When the first shots ring off, I instantly duck and cringe while hiding my face in Tony's chest. He puts his other hand around my lower back and holds me close. Everyone else seems to huddle closer to me in fear and I struggle to keep my powers going. My body starts feeling weak. I'm not sure if it's the fact I am sharing my power of invisibility with all of these people that is draining me or the fact that I can feel the fear permeating through their pores and into mine.

I look back up to find that the 'soldiers' are grabbing people and shooting them point blank with their weapons. My heart begins to race knowing my parents are out there somewhere. I can't for the life of me figure out how they'll escape.

With all the worry and anxiety that is flooding through my veins, and with the added stress of keeping this many people invisible, I begin to weaken more and more. I close my eyes and pray that my parents are going to be okay. As soon as I open them though, I see that my prayer has not been answered. To my horror, I watch as my parents struggle against two armed men who have them each in a chokehold. I watch as they point a smaller gun at their necks. Tony must see what I'm seeing because his hand covers my mouth the second I am about to let out a panicked scream.

I hear a gunshot—maybe it was two—and watch as my parents fall to the ground in a heap. Tears sting my eyes as I try to convince myself that this isn't happening. The urge to run to them is so great that I can barely contain it.

Tony glances over at me, his face red with fury, and asks me if I'm okay. I don't know how to respond so I don't; I just try to tell him with my eyes what my heart wants so badly to say. It wants to say that I am in utter disbelief; I just saw both of my parents shot point blank a few yards in front of me. All of this heartache, combined with the people around me who are draining my powers, makes me instantly weak. My head drops a few inches as I rest it on the top of Lily's head.

Tony asks me again in a more intense whisper, "Willow, are you okay? Answer me!"

My eyes begin closing against my will. Between the slits of my closing eyelids, I see a pair of men in black coming our way. I can't let go now. They will surely see us if I do.

"Willow," Tony whispers again, looking from me back to the men who are gaining on us.

"My…powers," is all I can manage to say. The men are only a few feet away now.

Suddenly, Tony lets go of my arm, turning visible. I want so badly to protest. I try to reach my hand out to grab him, but my arm doesn't move, it's too weak. He can't let go… he'll get himself killed!

Tony leans over me very briefly and says, "I can see your powers slipping. Please get these people to safety. I'm going to see if I can help your parents. God willing, I will see you again." He kisses the top of my head and runs towards the men. I try to say something to stop him, but I'm just not strong enough. He tackles the men to the ground effectively and manages to keep from getting shot. I begin hoping against hope that he can make it through this.

I use all the energy I have to keep the people around me safe, while Tony works to lure the other soldiers away from our hiding place. All I can do is watch helplessly as person after person is shot and falls to the ground. Tony reaches the area where my parents lie. He bends down and looks at them, then looks back in the direction where we hide. His expression seems perplexed and I wish I could hear what he's trying to tell me with that look.

Another soldier walks up behind Tony. I want to call out to him but it happens so fast. All too soon, I watch as Tony becomes the newest victim and falls slowly to the ground next to my parents.

A scream wells up inside my throat as I watch two of the 'soldiers' drag their lifeless bodies into the back of an SUV. No! Everything that I love is being ripped away from me. I want to move—I want to go after them—but I couldn't even if I had the energy to do so. The lives of fifteen other people depend on me.

About ten more minutes go by before all the victims and soldiers have been piled into the trucks. The doors securely close them inside. The helicopters lift away as the SUV's peel off down a dirt path, leaving nothing but a cloud of dust in their wake. I feel myself falling though a dark tunnel, Tony's name whispered on my lips as I lose consciousness.

Run! It's all I can think to do at a time like this.

My mind can't comprehend why he would be chasing me or why he has murder in his eyes. I run behind an alley that lines a steel graveyard of refineries and old buildings. The sound of his feet hitting the pavement behind me propels me forward. My eyes must be glowing neon yellow with how hard I'm pushing this ability.

"Don't worry, Willow! I'm not going to hurt you." His breath doesn't even sound winded. I don't dare glance behind me, not even when he adds an evil, "much," to the end of that sentence a second later.

A few yards ahead, there is a fork in the road. I debate whether I should take it or stay on this straight path. At the last possible second I decide to go for it. I push the limits of my power, running so ridiculously fast that I can only imagine there's a smoke trail under my sneakers. I take the turn and the pit in my stomach bottoms out. Wrong freaking move!

He laughs from behind me as I come to a standstill in front of a brick wall. My hands meet it and grip into the grooves of the grout holding the bricks together. There was a time that his laugh would have comforted me. Not today. No, that laugh has an edge to it that tells me he no longer is in control of his actions. He's the marionette for a powerful puppet master. I should have killed that jerk when I had the chance! I turn around slowly with my head to the ground. I don't know if my heart can take seeing him.

"Please," I say, before I lift my head up to meet his glare. My breath catches as I take him in and my heart betrays me by perking up at the sight of him. So many emotions run through me and no words can express the way I feel. Something incomprehensible tells me that even if I die at his hand, I will not hate him. There is no such fortune for me to be able to hate the man who haunts my dreams and hunts me in the night. His copper hair shines under the moonlight and his eyes glow an eerie burgundy red, swirling together with hints of yellow. There is evil in those eyes. Not an internal evil, but one that has been forced upon him. I don't mean for my plea to come out in a throaty whisper, one that begs him to see me, but it does. I need him to see through everything that has been done to him, to us, and to break away from the one who pulls his strings. It comes out as I plead, "Please, Tony."

๛

As if adrenaline has been pumped into my veins, I shoot up from the bed, gasping for air. I look around the room and expect to see him in front of me. I have no idea where I am. I push my fingers through my sweaty hair as my eyes try to focus in the minimal light. What was that?

A dream? A premonition?

A door opens and candlelight filters in through its crack. "Willow?" The door opens wider and I watch Alec step into the room.

"Alec?" I blink a few times not sure what's going on. "Where am I?" I ask.

"You're in the new safe house; everything's going to be okay. We managed to get everyone here and situated while you were out. What you did back at the mountain took a great deal out of you, but you saved a lot of people. They are all calling you a hero." He steps closer to the bed. Something in his expression seems torn, but I'm not sure if it's just my imagination.

"Oh," is all I can think to say as I focus on withdrawing my memories from the far recesses of my mind. As if hitting me like a bullet, it all comes back to me. The mountain, the shooting, Zack and his dad, the soldiers, my parents and then Tony. The last two thoughts feel more like a landmine blew up in my heart than a bullet. Tony sacrificed himself for me, trying to save my parent's lives, even though they had already been lost.

"Are you feeling okay?" Alec asks me. I can see clearly now that there is a hesitancy about him that I can't quite explain. He seems hurt and conflicted. His hands keep clenching and unclenching as if he wants to reach out and touch me but he has to hold back. Something is definitely wrong.

I move my legs to the side of the bed, intending to stand up. I still feel weak so I lean back against the headboard. "Yes, I think so." I look up to Alec. "I need to find Tony and my parents," I tell him strongly. Even if they are all dead, I need to see them. It's as if I am trying to comprehend what happened at the mountain... it doesn't feel real.

Alec takes a step back; a hurt look overcomes his expression. "You were calling for him in your sleep you know."

I remember the dream I had right before waking up. It seemed so real. Those feelings I felt were vivid and unexplainable. I open my mouth but don't really know what to say. I try to divert his previous statement. "My parents. I think they're dead." The moment I say it aloud, it becomes a reality. I try to stifle a sob. "And Tony... I think he's dead too." I put my face in my hands, squeezing tight, trying to make the pain go away.

Alec comes to my side and crouches down beside me. "Willow, please stop crying and listen to me."

I can't for the life of me figure out why he is acting so blasé about the death of three people that I care so deeply about. He takes my chin in his hand and lifts my face so I can see him. I am instantly lost in his beautifully haunting, dark blue eyes, and a sense of peace moves over me. "They're not dead, Willow. The guns the 'soldiers' were carrying were loaded with special bullets that contained tranquilizers. It apparently knocks them out just long enough to get them transported to wherever they are going."

My heart begins hammering in my chest. My parents, Tony, they're alive? I think it to myself over and over again. It's as if grief and elation are fighting an internal battle inside me. I can't grasp my mind around it.

As if to reassure me that I heard him correctly Tony states, "Willow, Tony and your parents are alive. One of our soldiers who escaped came and told us what happened. He was able to tell us that, along with information about where they are keeping them locked up."

I take a moment to wrap my mind around everything Alec just said. I'm sure my mother and father are going to be okay, especially if they're together. For goodness sakes, my mother has been leading one of the largest militias around for the past several months. She can handle her own. Tony, however, I can't be sure. He's strong and smart but my heart is tugging at my feet to move and find him immediately. I have an uneasy feeling about his fate.

I voice this to Alec, "I need to find Tony."

Alec looks flustered the moment I say it aloud. "Look, Willow." Alec runs his hand through his hair.

Worried about what he's going to express, I cut him off, "He saved us! We can't leave him. I have to help him. And I have to help my parents too."

My words seem to wound Alec even more and that ricochets back onto me. I don't want to hurt Alec. Can't he just see that I have to help Tony and my parents? He seems to be at a loss for words, so I muster my strength and stand up. I start to walk past him towards the door. "I have to help them."

Alec grabs my arm and prevents me from reaching

the door. I turn to face him.

"I have to go, Alec." I plead with him to understand. I have no idea how long I've been out, but I know that any amount of time is too long. I need to find the person who knows where they're being kept. God only knows what they're going through right now.

Alec's eyes heat with a fire I haven't seen before. "You have to go? Just like you had to go in the middle of the night? You left me with your little brother. You left without saying a word!" His hand on my arm seems to squeeze a little harder. "We have sent a search team to retrieve all of our people, Willow. There's no need for you to go on a suicide mission!"

I take a deep breath, knowing he's right to be upset. "I know, Alec. I'm sorry, I am. I feel like it's my responsibility to rescue them though. I felt like I had to do it back then too."

"You didn't trust me to tell me your plans or to have me go with you the first time. But you trusted him?" Alec spits out the last word. He looks royally pissed.

"It's not about trust!" I yank my arm free from his and tuck my hair behind my ears. "Look, I don't have time for this right now. I have to go."

"You don't have time for me?" he asks.

I huff, not sure what else to do. I have to mentally make myself not stomp my foot. "It's not that I don't have time for you. I have a duty to help them. Tony saved me and I at least owe him the same respect in return."

"Who are you trying to kid, Willow? It's more

obvious than the nose on your face. You have more than a duty to help Tony! I see the way you look at him and the way he looks at you." His voice grows quiet as he takes a deep breath, holding my stare with his.

My face falls as the realization of what he's saying dawns on my heart. I want to say that I have no idea what he's talking about, but the turmoil I've been feeling around Tony, and the memories of my feelings in that dream, can't be denied. I look back up at Alec, torn, not sure what to say.

"Willow, I can't handle this. You obviously don't trust me enough to confide in me and..."

I cut him off. "I do trust you!" A helpless feeling settles in as I feel something starting to slip away that I so desperately want to hold onto.

"I honestly don't think you do, at least not completely. Look, you will always hold a special place in my heart, but I can't keep competing for a battle that's already won."

I furrow my brow at him. "What battle, Alec?" The frustration has my heart speeding up.

"The battle for your heart, Willow." The emotion in his eyes is like a kick to my gut.

My stomach drops. "What?" I reach out to grab his hand and he yanks it away from me. The hurt from that simple action stings like a bee and my eyes instinctively tear up. "I don't know what you're talking about, Alec."

"I think you do, Willow, you just haven't admitted it to yourself yet. Tell me that everything I'm saying or thinking is wrong. Tell me that I must be insane and losing my mind. Tell me that, please," he whispers as he looks away from me.

"I..." I don't know what to say. What can I say that wouldn't be a lie? I have no idea what I feel. I open my mouth but no more words come out. How can I sit here and not declare that he is so far from the truth? Why can't I just say two simple words? You're wrong. Those two words can stop what's about to happen from happening. Nothing comes to my lips though, and I dread what's coming next.

"See, you can't even deny it. I can't do this." His voice is choked with emotion.

I close my eyes in that moment and swallow hard. I drop my head again, unable to look him in the eye. A tear slips down my cheek as I realize what's about to come. "So, this is it?" I ask Alec. I look up at him and my emotions are threatening to burst like a dam that's too full of water.

Alec runs his fingers through his hair and then he looks into my eyes one last time before nodding in affirmation. He takes the three steps to the door, leaves, and closes it behind him without ever looking back.

I don't have it in me to think about what just occurred, but it only takes a few moments before the dam breaks and my eyes flood with tears. They spill down my cheeks and onto the bed. I hold my head in my hands, rocking back and forth. I feel so unattached from the world, like what I'm living right now isn't even real. I can't distinguish truth from reality. All that I ever knew has been ripped from me... it's as if this was the straw that broke the camel's back.

I grab the pillow next to me and place it over my

face. I sob into it loudly, hoping not to draw attention to myself, but also desperately trying to release these foreign emotions. I scream and sob into the pillow, desperate for some sort of relief.

I hear the door click back open and I peek over the pillow to see Claire standing in the doorway. She wastes no time in coming to my side. "Alec said you might need me." She wraps her arms around my middle and draws me close to her small frame. I cry on her shoulder as she strokes my hair. It reminds me of something my mother would do.

"It hurts," I tell her, as I clutch at my heart that feels as if it's breaking into a million sad little pieces.

"I know. It will be okay, I promise." She strokes my hair some more. "It will all be okay."

As my sobs turn into a softer cry, she places her hands on each of my arms and lifts me from her embrace. She wipes the tears from my cheeks and hands me a tissue. I gladly accept it and dab at my nose.

"I know you may not believe me now," Claire begins. "But this heartache you're experiencing will soon be but a memory… one that won't hurt near as bad as it currently does."

I'm tempted to ask her how she could possibly know that, when I remember what Claire's life has been like. She lost both of her parents very young in life. If anything, her loss is far worse than mine is.

I wrap my arms back around her, hoping that she isn't reliving the pain of her past for my expense. "Thank you," I whisper into her ear. I don't need to say anything more to her. I can tell she already knows how thankful I am to have her as a friend. She's always there in my time of need and goodness knows I will always be there for her.

"Why don't you go get washed up? You are probably starving!" Claire pats my leg.

I shake my head. "No, I need to find the soldier who knows where they are keeping my parents and Tony."

"Why?" She looks at me and then shakes her head in understanding. "Look, Willow. They already sent a team to save them. I know they will get them out. You can't go. Not by yourself."

"How long ago did they leave?" I wonder if I can catch up with them.

"This morning; that's over four hours ago. You can't catch up with them," she says as if answering my unasked question.

"Now look whose reading minds," I tell her. "Actually, I can catch up with them. I'm mighty fast. They're probably carrying heavy artillery. I won't be needing near as much as they do. Now, who's the guy I need to see?"

Claire looks down uncomfortably and fidgets with her nails. "I don't think I should say." CRAP! THAT'S A SUICIDE MISSION. ALEC WOULD BE PISSED IF I TOLD HER IT WAS THAT JOSH GUY. As if sensing my invasion, she darts her head up and meets my eyes. "How dare you!"

I cringe at her angry glare. "I'm sorry, Claire. I have to help them. I know you don't understand but I can't just sit around and wait to see if the rescue team accomplishes their mission. I have to go." I feel bad for betraying Claire's trust, but I have no other options right now. I stand up and catch my reflection in the mirror above the bed. My eyes are a dark green. This eye color corresponding to my abilities thing sucks. There's no way to be covert at all.

"Fine! Then I'm coming with you!" She stands up and throws her hands on her hips.

"Absolutely not." There is no way I'm going to let anything happen to any more of the people I love.

"This isn't up for discussion. I'm coming," she demands.

I focus on her eyes. "No. You are not coming. You are not going to tell anyone else that I know about Josh. You won't follow me or even remember that we had this conversation. Do you understand?"

Her eyes glaze over a bit as she nods her head. "I understand."

"Thank you." I take a deep breath. My heart is hammering out of my chest and bile is rising into my throat. I can't believe I'm doing this to my best friend. I once again feel as if I am left with no other choice. "I love you, Claire. I'm sorry," I tell her.

Her eyes focus again. "What are you sorry for, sweetie?"

I sigh. "Everything." She looks even more confused so I add, "I think I'll wash up before going down to eat. You don't have to wait for me though."

She hesitates but finally shrugs her shoulders. "Okay. I'll leave my light with you. This hotel is set up much like the other one. The dining hall is downstairs. I'll see you in a few."

"Okay." I pull her into a big hug and hold on firmly. It takes a lot to blink back the tears that invade my eyes. I let her go, she hands me her candle and then leaves the room.

I take a moment to wash my face. The hazel eyes of a girl who's becoming more and more like a stranger, stare back at me. The same hazel eyes that Zack has... I mean had.

I grab a new pair of jeans and a tank top from the dresser and change quickly. Then I head out in search of Josh. The hallways are deserted; probably because everyone is eating. I pass a room on my way to the dining hall and stop quickly. The door is slightly open, but from here, I can tell that it's the weapons room.

I slowly push back the door and my lantern illuminates the small, conference style room. I half expect to see Tony inside waiting for me. The crater in my chest throbs a little more. I'm not sure if it's caused by my worry over Tony and my parents, my betrayal of my best friend's trust or the fact that Alec and I just broke up.

I take a few deep breaths and focus on pushing away these emotions. This is no time to be weak. I look around the room and grab two small pistols, a knife, and some ammo. I stuff everything into a small backpack, and start walking towards the dining hall.

I stop along the way when I see an exit sign. I turn down the short hallway and look around before opening the door. I shiver. The night air outside is crisp and cool. I'm still amazed at how much the government failed in its plan to heat the Earth. I place my backpack outside to the right of the door, and then head back inside.

When I turn from the hallway, I bump into someone and lose my balance. He grabs my arm and steadies me. My heart beats double time as I look up at Alec. "I'm sorry," I whisper.

"Me too," he whispers back.

We stare at each other and, for a moment, I think about saying, I'm sorry, I love you, please forgive me. I don't though and it's awkward. The moment passes when Connor walks up. I turn my attention towards him.

"Hey, Willow! I'm so glad you're okay." He pulls me into a Connor-sized bear hug.

"Thanks, Connor." I smile up at him.

He looks over at Alec and then back at me. The awkwardness is evident. "So, how about that dinner? Chicken and dumplings. Yum!"

"Oh? I'm just heading there," I tell him.

"You better hurry. They are running low," Connor says.

"Yeah, after you ate like five servings!" I hadn't heard Claire approach. She playfully jabs at Connor's shoulder.

"I can't help it. I'm a growing boy." He leans down and gives her a quick kiss.

I look away and end up meeting Alec's gaze. My face heats up and I have to avert my eyes again.

"Well, I better go grab some food before more

growing boys get at it," I try to joke but the smile doesn't come.

Claire gives me a sympathetic grin. "Do you want me to go with you?"

"No, it's fine. I'm just going to go grab a bite and then I may go to bed early. I'm feeling really tired." Argh! I freaking hate lying.

Alec moves a little and I can't help but look up at him. He's studying me like he doesn't believe me.

I decide this is the best time to make my exit. "Alright, I better go."

"Goodnight," Connor and Claire say.

I walk past them, making sure not to look at Alec. I don't get but two steps away before someone grabs my elbow.

He gently jerks me around to face him. "You aren't planning anything stupid, are you?" Alec studies my eyes.

I look down at his hand on my arm and the close proximity to him makes my insides stir. I'm so close that I could easily stand on my tiptoes and pull him into a kiss. I could make everything better. Why am I not doing it? I slowly shake my head. "No," I answer him.

He stares me down for a few more seconds and then he lets go of my arm; I turn and walk quickly away in the opposite direction. The butterflies that once fluttered free toss and turn in my stomach in utter confusion.

I'll be surprised if I still have any friends left after this. As soon as I get out of their eyesight I double back to look for the man with the intel. Before I round a corner, I hear a couple talking. I stop dead in my tracks, desperately trying not to draw attention. I can't help but listen to their banter while I wait for the coast to be clear.

"Clarissa, you know that I've had a thing for you for a while right?" The man's voice takes on a sultry tone. I cringe, hoping I'm not about to witness something embarrassing.

"I've kinda figured that out only recently," she says back to him while chewing loudly on a piece of gum. "I asked my friend if she knew who kept sending the flowers that never had a note attached. She said she was pretty sure she knew who it was but that she wouldn't tell me. I was so mad at her because I couldn't for the life of me figure it out."

I roll my eyes, hoping this playful badgering doesn't take up too much more of my time. I need to find Josh and get the heck out of dodge! I look up to the ceiling and see a mirror attached to the corner of the wall. No doubt it was put there so that people wouldn't run into each other when they rounded the sharp turn. I let my mind wander for a second. I bet it would be pretty funny if they put a camera behind it, I think to myself. The things it would see. I guess it wouldn't matter without electricity though. I squelch a small giggle from myself and focus on the two of them around the corner. From what I can tell from here, the guy is standing pretty close to the girl and he is twirling her hair in his fingers. She's blushing and looking at her shoes. Oh brother.

"So," Clarissa begins again. "I took my friend's locket and hid it in my room and told her she couldn't have it back until she spilled the beans on who sent the flowers."

"Uh-huh," he says, egging her on. "And what did she have to say?" Although by now, the answer is completely obvious.

"Well," she says with a giggle. "She said many unladylike things about my stealing the locket. Then she finally said: You silly…Josh sent them."

My mouth drops open, realizing that the Josh I need to talk may very well be standing on the other side of this hallway. How convenient! I quickly formulate a plan on how to interrupt this…whatever you call it, without making a scene. I back up a few paces and jiggle a door handle. I watch in the mirror as the two of them gain about an extra foot of distance between them. I walk heavy to make sure they know I'm coming around the corner. They stand casually next to each other as if it's just normal, everyday behavior.

"Oh, hey guys," I say, breaking the ice.

"Hey," they say back in unison.

"Josh right?" I ask, even though I already know. He nods his head but the girl looks at me like I'm trying to take her man. Down girl, I think to myself. "One of the soldiers said that he spoke with you at the meeting earlier about the reconnaissance mission, you know, where they're keeping the other soldiers locked up." I'm totally shooting in the dark here but hoping I hit a bull's eye. He doesn't stop me so I continue. "Sorry, I can't remember his name…" I leave the sentence hanging while snapping my fingers, hoping he'll fill in the blank.

"You mean Steve?" he fills in, looking annoyed.

Bingo! "Yes, Steve," I say with a little too much exuberance. "Steve wanted to see if you could draw up a simple map so he can show it to some of the others about where the location is that the prisoners are being held at." Yes, I know that this is probably going to end up badly, but I'm hoping that he just wants me out of his hair so he can get back to Clarissa. The fastest way for him to do that is to give me what I want.

He eyes me kind of funny for a moment but slowly pulls a pen out of his shirt pocket. "Steve said that?"

I nod my head in affirmation. "He told me to tell you that some of the details of the plan were lost to him. He was wondering if you could do this so it'll jar his memory." Josh shakes his head.

"Man, that old fart always forgets stuff. Why Alice put him in charge I'll never know."

I give him a small smile. "Yeah, he did seem a bit off, if you know what I mean," I say, to try to be more personal.

"Clarissa, do you have a piece of paper or something?" I know he asked her but I search through my pockets anyway and come up empty.

Lo and behold, she pulls out a business card sized piece of paper from her bra. Josh turns an unnatural shade of red and carefully takes the paper from her as if it's the most precious piece of paper in the world.

Ick, I think I just gagged! By the way they exchange shy, yet ogling, glances, I can only assume that the card must be one of the blank ones that he put on the flowers he sent her.

It takes him a few moments to roughly sketch a map of some sort onto the business card. He hands it to me and says, "Here you go." I can also catch the other thing he didn't have to say out loud, here's what you came for, now leave.

I smile and walk past them, thanking them for their time. I round another corner happy to be away from that sick love fest. I don't think I could have handled any more of that. The romance was palpable in the air… like you could cut it with a knife. I stick the card in my back pocket, noticing that it doesn't have any sort of direction or compass on it.

I think I can figure out a way to decipher the map though. I come back around to the exit sign, silently and stealthily slink out the door, and close it quietly behind me, making sure it latches. I pick up my bag and toss it over my shoulders. I stretch my arms above my head and look around, trying to gather my bearings.

I spot a fire escape ladder hanging from the side of the hotel. I unlatch it and flinch at the loud squeak it lets out. I hold it in midair, making sure that I'm still undetected. After a few seconds, I let the ladder down the rest of the way and set it quietly on the ground. I grab the metal sides and begin making my way up the numerous series of ladders, to the top of the roof. The wind whips across my face the higher I get up. Instead of the trepidation I thought I would feel at these heights, I feel rejuvenated and energized… like I'm on top of the world.

I reach the top of the ladder and carefully make my way onto the gravel-paved roof. There's a few old air conditioners and other machinery here I can't identify. I watch my step, making sure I don't trip. It's a little creepy that there's no railing, but I guess no one is really supposed to be up here in the first place.

I saunter over to the middle of the roof and set my backpack down. Scanning the horizon, I take a mental note of any particular landmarks that are around me. I pull out the piece of paper and hold it so the moon's reflection allows me to see what's written. Glancing this way and that, I try to match up what's drawn on the paper with what's out there. Then I see it, to the east, a small glow dotting the horizon. I'm not sure if it's where they took Tony and my parents but it's the only light that's illuminating the sky… besides the moon and stars that is. I point the piece of paper in that direction and sure enough, it's an exact match for where I need to go.

I glance back up and focus in on the small glow that's illuminated in the distance. It's strange to see what must be electricity being used. That definitely has Dr. Hastings written all over it. Who else would manage to find a way to turn the power on? Thoughts of government conspiracies pass through my mind. I wonder if they have any knowledge of what's going on here or if this is all at their discretion. I sure hope not, because if so, I may be headed into a battle I have no chance of winning.

I take a few more seconds to note what's between

the place I'm headed and me; then I grab my things and head back down.

Once safely on the ground, I take a deep breath and start to run. I run as fast as my body will take me down an abandoned paved road. I figure if I stick to solid ground, that I could cover more distance than if I traveled in the trees. It does mean more risk of being seen, but I have to take that chance if I want to get to Tony and my parents as soon as possible.

For the longest time all I hear is the clap, clap of my shoes hitting the hard ground. I run against the wind and it gratefully pulls the hair away from my face. For a moment I feel like I am back in that dream I had only a few hours before... except this time I'm racing to save Tony instead of being hunted by him. The thought makes me shiver and I immediately relinquish it.

I run for what seems like hours, mentally checking off in my head the landmarks as I pass them. An old abandoned gas station, a rest stop, a tiny Wal-Mart, and then a fork in the road. I curve off to my left and come around a corner.

After a few more miles, I begin to see small slivers of light through the trees on my left. I take this as my cue to get off the road and into the woods. I slow my pace, scared that my speed may work faster than my brain. The last thing I need is to catapult myself into a tree and knock myself out.

I slow down to a jog and then to a steady walk. I want to try to rest my powers before I attempt to use them again. Goodness only knows what waits for me behind those trees. Hopefully, it's the place I need to go.

With no advanced warning, a hand wraps around my mouth and waist. I try to scream and struggle away but to no avail. Then a voice whispers in my ear, "Shhh, it's me…Tom."

It takes me a moment before my body registers that Tom isn't an enemy but an ally. In fact, he's part of the fab four my mother assigned to protect me early on when we went on smaller missions. When he feels my body go lax, he lets go of his death grip and turns me around to face him. I squint in the darkness and see him holding his index finger over his lips. I nod my head in understanding of his signal to stay quiet. He grabs me by the hand, leads me over to a small group of trees, and has me squat down next to him. "I don't know how on earth you found us," he whispers. "But the fact is you're here and we could use an extra set of hands… er powers. Right now, our team is doing reconnaissance. We are meeting up in twenty to define our plan of attack."

I nod my head in understanding. "What have you observed so far?"

"You see over there," he points to an opening in the trees. I look over at a large brick wall with barbed wire affixed to the top. While I can't see beyond the fence, I can see the light from within its perimeter shining out. Seeing electricity on the 'outside' still seems unreal. "Inside that facility is where they're keeping them."

I'm guessing he's meaning all the people that were

seized next to the mountainside, including my parents and Tony. My spirits lift a bit at the realization that they're so close… yet so far. The wall and barbed wire looks vicious. "Do you know how many there are on the other side?" I ask.

He shakes his head.

Nerves start setting in as I stare at the wall. I have all of these comic worthy powers, where the heck is the x-ray vision when I need it? If I weren't so scared right now, I'd probably laugh at that joke. My hands begin to sweat and I wipe them on my pants. I whisper, "How are they keeping those people locked up now that all of their powers are unleashed? Why wouldn't some of them just walk through walls or go invisible and escape?"

I watch Tom shrug. "One can only wonder what they're going through in there."

Thoughts of kryptonite pass through my head. If Dr. Hastings had a device that took down Reapers, what might he have in store for everyone else? I shiver at the thought of metal chains and steel bars holding those people prisoner. Feeling helpless with the endless possibilities, I make sure my mind doesn't digress into the what-if's. Instead, I take control of what I can do. "What can I do to help?"

"We will know more when we meet up with the others. I think that your many abilities will come in handy. Other than our kind, we have a few people with us who can go invisible, a few who can walk through walls and some healers. Since you can do all of the above, we can place you anywhere. Your compulsion may come in handy too," he whispers.

"I'll do anything, just as long as I get to go inside," I declare. I know I'm going inside no matter what, but I can't help but think about how hard my mom and the others worked to protect me from the Reapers. I don't want them to continue in that trend in this instance… especially since we aren't dealing with Reapers here. I refuse to stand on the sidelines any longer.

"Don't worry about that. We'll take all the people we can get if we expect to pull this off," Tom says. Without another word, he signals for me to follow him.

We stealthily maneuver through the tree line that encircles the prison. At one point, the only thing standing between the prison and us is an electric fence. I have no idea if it's electrified but I don't plan on finding out. We do get a good view of the prison yard. The prison itself is two stories tall with small, barred windows dotting the grey brick exterior. The makings of it look cold and hard.

An armed guard makes his rounds along the inside perimeter. Tom and I stay in the same spot for a few minutes to see if there is a routine. Every three minutes the guard passes by. He must be walking back and forth, back and forth. Tom takes out a pair of binoculars and takes note of all the guard's eye colors he can see. We aren't sure if they have abilities, but we need to be prepared just in case. It's best to just assume that they do for now.

Realizing it's time for the rendezvous, we head towards the rally point. About a quarter a mile up the road, we meet up with the others. I count about fifty people in all. Around three-fourths of the soldiers have yellow eyes and the last quarter of the group is a mix between purple, navy, and brown eyes.

What surprises me most is the man that steps to the front of the group. Mr. Leroy. He eyes me and nods his head in acceptance of my being present. First, he asks for feedback on what everyone saw. Each designated leader of the different reconnaissance teams takes turns relaying information. They refer to Dr. Hastings's soldiers as Unfriendlies. I'm amazed at how organized the information is relayed from person to person. So far, we know that there are fifteen Unfriendlies guarding the outside perimeter of the prison. We still don't know what's on the inside.

After hearing more about the approximate layout of the prison, Mr. Leroy speaks up. "We will split up into teams with at least one person who can turn invisible, one who can walk through walls and one who can heal on each team. We will have four teams total. Our goal is to get in and stay invisible for as long as you can. Look around; find out how they are keeping everyone contained. Look for any weaknesses or ways to escape. You must know that this mission is for reconnaissance only." Mr. Leroy turns his attention on me for the last part of his speech. "You are not to engage in combat at all on the inside. Go in and look around. Get a feel for the layout and get out. Our goal is to remain undetected. If they know we are in there, we will lose our advantage and they may beef up security or worse, they may come looking for the shelter where we're keeping all the children." I involuntarily shiver. "We'll meet back at this rally point in one hour. If we find that the situation is something we can take on our own, without reinforcements, then we will lay out more plans. Please split off into teams."

Mr. Leroy allows the team leaders to work out the arrangements as he heads over to speak with me one-on-one. "I'm glad you're here, Willow."

I raise my eyebrow at him in surprise. "Really?" For some reason it seemed like the last thing he would say.

He seems to ponder the question as if it's a surprise to him as well. "Well, yes. Your powers are very useful. What won't be helpful though, is your emotional tie to this situation."

"This isn't a situation, Lee." He jerks back in surprise. We've never been on a first name basis... at least not until now. "This is about my parents and Tony," I emphasize.

"I understand, Willow. At this point, we could be walking into a blood bath. We have to get information first to figure out how to proceed. I need to know that I can trust you not to do anything rash."

I lie, "I won't." He is about to walk away but I stop him. "Why are you leading this? I thought you just wanted to leave and escape. That you didn't want to fight," I state, recalling the night before the Reaper attacked the shelter. Mr. Leroy, along with more than half of my mother's group, was planning to break away and go to the new safe house. They were ready to abandon the mission of keeping the shelter safe in order to keep themselves safe. I understand the parents of the children making that decision, but not people like Mr. Leroy who seemingly had nothing to lose.

"You may not believe that Mr. Grumps-a-lot

has friends, but I do." My eyes widen when I hear him acknowledge the name I used to call him behind his back. He brushes off my acknowledgement and continues. "Most of them are inside that prison; including your mom and your dad. They didn't ask to be captured. Whatever is going on here just upped the stakes. It's no longer about a war on Reapers. We may be fighting something a whole lot bigger and I have a duty to protect and serve."

By the way he declared his last statement, I wonder if he's ex-military. "I respect that." I say it because I do.

"Good. Then respect my orders when I say that you are not to show yourself to anyone or try to break anyone out until we rally back and make a more precise game plan." He stands firm, awaiting my assurance.

"Fine," I say. Yeah right! If I see my family and Tony, you better believe I will be busting them out of there. It's not likely that three people gone will be noticed. It's like leaving a pile of unopened Halloween candy in front of a child and telling them that they can only look at it... but not eat it.

He tries to give me a hard stare with his yellow eyes to reinforce his orders. I don't back down, so after a few seconds he nods and excuses himself to meet with the other team leaders.

After a few minutes, we are all split into teams of around thirteen people. My heart is pounding as the adrenaline pumps through my veins. I can hardly contain myself as I wait for the others in my group to get their guns and ammo together. One of the soldiers must see my fidgeting because I feel a hand steady my bopping shoulder. I take a deep breath and give him some semblance of a smile. His hand leaves my shoulder, taking away the warm comfort he provided.

As luck should have it, Mr. Leroy… or Lee as I have come to call him, is the leader of the group I'm in. Oh goodie, I think to myself in a sarcastic manner. If I have any chance of getting what I need, which is my parents and Tony, I can't be around Lee. I'm going to have to separate from him and go AWOL, hoping the others don't take notice.

Thankfully, there is one more person that can go invisible and one that can pass through walls in our group. So, if I do leave it won't be like they can't get out, I tell myself. We form a line, each person holding the person's shoulder in front of them. I use my invisibility and so does the person towards the front. It still feels draining, but not near as much as if I had to do it all on my own. I made sure I was near the back for good reason… Lee is in the front.

We do a short, very quiet march to the barbed wire fence. I can feel the intensity of emotions in the group and I do my best to ignore them. I don't blame them when they stiffen up as a guard looks our way. Thankfully, the guard has purple eyes. It's difficult to get your brain to understand that the guard can't see you. The only real enemy here would be the blue-eyed people, those with Candy's gift.

We pass through the fence uneventfully. The lights are on all around us, which makes it look like daytime. It's a bonus for us because we can at least see the one thing that tells of someone's ability… their eyes.

We quickly run the perimeter of the yard and stop when we get to a darkened corner. I try not to let my guard down because I know all of these people depend on me and the other dude to keep us invisible. To be honest though, the guards that walk the perimeter and those stationed high above us, give me the heebie-jeebies with their large weapons that point where they're looking. I give an involuntary shiver as we near the inner brick wall, which most likely houses all of the people from the mountain.

A brown-eyed man helps me get each soldier through the wall. We start with the man who can keep everyone invisible.

I'm the last to cross through, and as soon as I do, my stomach threatens to lose whatever little sustenance it has inside it. All around our feet are people still in their scrubs, as well as a few of our soldiers. They lay lifeless on the floor, drooling from their mouths. I reach down quickly, still holding onto the person in front of me, and check for a pulse. It's weak but it's still there.

The room is relatively small, maybe ten feet wide and ten feet long. We stand there staring at the carnage, awaiting instructions from Lee. I look around at all the faces, some slightly familiar from life in the mountain. There are some I've spoken with when I was a Runner or just seen passing by in my daily routes. I think I see my teacher somewhere in the corner so I turn away. I can't get distracted from the real reason I'm here.

Sadly, I don't see my parents or Tony in this room.

One person in particular makes me queasy; it's the woman from the first day my father and I arrived at the shelter. She's the one that, while standing in line for our meal, told us that this was all a conspiracy and we're going to die. I don't think she's crazy anymore, that's for sure.

Seeing that prisoners, not Unfriendlies, occupy this room, Lee steps away from the person behind him, becoming visible. He motions for us to drop our hands and all of us become visible too. I reluctantly drop my hand from the person in front of me. Lee quickly instructs us about what to do. "I want you all to try and find out why these people are like this. Work quickly and quietly so we remain undetected. If you suspect someone is about to open the door and enter, you all need to run to the wall over there." He points in the direction of the northerly wall. "Invisibility people, you need to immediately grab as many people as you can. If for some reason you can't make it then you need to lie down and remain motionless." We nod our heads and get to work.

I walk over to the woman that makes my toes curl and examine her. She looks normal except for the vacant expression she exhibits. I look over all the visual parts of her body and see nothing out of place. There must be something that is causing them to be like this, I think to myself.

I listen into her thoughts but all I hear are jumbled words that make no sense whatsoever. After listening to her for a little while longer though, I hear two words that come up often… 'arm' and 'hurt'.

I look down at her arms but don't see anything unusual at first glance. I roll up her sleeve and hit something with my hand. A small white patch sticks to the fleshy part of her arm. I run my fingers over it and feel a strange sensation go through my body. It looks like some sort of an adhesive is holding it in place. I decide to attempt to remove it. I remember my dad always telling me when I was younger to make sure I rip the bandage off instead of spending the time to pick it off little by little. So that's what I do. I rip it off and I'm startled by the moan the woman makes. I look down at her arm where the bandage once was and see hundreds of teeny-tiny pinprick dots of blood.

I look back at the bandage and realize that the bottom of it is filled with hundreds of short needles. I have to fight the gagging sensation that comes with the sight of this. It looks so otherworldly, not like anything I've ever seen.

I make eye contact with Lee and motion him over to me. I show him the bandage and the spot where it was on her arm.

He checks another person's arm beside me and, lo and behold, there's another bandage on their arm, identical to this one. He quickly removes it and examines it as well.

While he's looking at it, I see the woman below me begin to stir and wake up. "Lee," I whisper.

He turns and witnesses her waking also. She seems extremely groggy so I place my hands on her and focus healing her. Color floods back into her cheeks and her eyes are no longer glazed over.

I put my finger up to my lip to do my best to calm her and tell her she can't scream. I bend down over her and whisper, "It's okay. I'm one of the good guys and we're trying to help you. Can you tell me anything about what's going on… anything that you remember?" I look at her with hope that maybe she can tell me where my parents and Tony are. The thought of them like this makes me want to hurl.

"They shot us. They killed us." She looks like she's about to start freaking out. "They shot us. They killed us." She keeps repeating this mantra over and over and is growing steadily higher in volume.

Maybe this wasn't the best person to try to get inside info from. I get as close as I can to her face so she will shut up and look into my eyes. "YOU NEED TO CALM DOWN AND NOT SAY ANOTHER WORD." Just like that, her eyes glaze over and she nods her head.

Lee gives me a funny look.

The other woman that Lee pulled the patch off of is starting to wake up too. I decide the best thing to do is to start straight off with compulsion. "YOU ARE SAFE. DON'T SCREAM. WE ARE HERE TO HELP YOU. YOU NEED TO HELP US FIRST THOUGH. TELL US EVERYTHING YOU SAW AND EVERYTHING YOU KNOW ABOUT WHAT HAS HAPPENED SINCE YOU WERE CAPTURED."

Her black eyes glaze over. Of all the gifts to have, feeling other's emotions right now would be the suckiest of all. She speaks in a monotone voice. "They shot us. When we woke up we were in a huge room filled with guards. They pricked our fingers and placed the blood on strips, which they ran through handheld machines. Sometimes the machine beeped. When that happened, they took the person out of the room at gunpoint. The machine didn't beep for me. The rest of us that remained in the room were scared. The guards came by one by one and placed a patch on each person's arm. They all fell down within seconds. I thought they were killing us." I can sense her emotions starting to rise.

"IT'S OKAY. YOU ARE NOT DEAD. YOU ARE SAFE. DO YOU KNOW WHAT THE TESTS WERE FOR? OR WHERE THEY TOOK THE OTHERS?" I doubt she knows but it's worth a shot.

She shakes her head. "We don't know what the tests were for or where the others went."

I have to fight off the frustration that builds. It's not like it's her fault that she doesn't know. I clench my hands into fists and stand up quickly.

Lee takes over my position, kneeling down by the woman. "Thank you for the information. You will need to follow our instructions to the dot to stay safe. Do you understand? We will do our best to get you out of here."

I steadily back away as I watch Lee continue to comfort the woman. Soon enough I find my back against the wall. Everyone in the room is busy looking elsewhere so I take my opportunity. I turn myself invisible and step through the wall.

I find myself in a dreary, grey-bricked hallway lit by

long rows of fluorescent tube lights. To say the decorating is cold and uninviting is an understatement. This is a place that you don't want to stick around for long, if at all. I move through the hallway, thankfully not running into any guards. Eventually the grey brick walls turn into barred jail cells. I look from side to side into each one expecting to find someone. They are all empty.

Hearing footsteps around a nearby corner, I step through the bars to hide in an empty cell. The bars offer little protection, but I'm not taking the chance on running into anyone who can see through abilities. A guard holding an assault rifle walks purposefully down the hallway.

The thought of him finding our people in that room, sends me into panic mode. I don't know if that's where his destination is but I have a duty to help them. I step quietly out into the hallway, reaching for the knife in the waistband of my pants. I speed up to where I'm right behind him. He turns around all of a sudden and looks right through me. I hold my breath. His eyes are copper like my dad's. I wonder if he saw this coming. I look down at my knife and back up at the guy who is about to turn back around. My heart hammers in my chest as I think about what I'm about to do.

I move closer to the man and raise the knife. That's when I feel it. His emotions. Something within him is torn. He despises himself and feels helpless at the same time. So many feelings go through him and into me. I slowly lower the knife, realizing that this guy is just a pawn. He doesn't deserve to die.

A lesson Tony taught me on knocking people out comes to mind. I move forward and wrap my arm around his throat so fast that he doesn't stand a chance. With his neck in the crook of my elbow like Tony showed me, I pull him off balance and he falls, with me underneath him. I didn't mean for that to happen but he is so much taller than I am. I do manage to keep my grip on him and squeeze my arm tighter. I'm hoping to block the artery on the side of his neck like I learned from Tony. I have to focus my strength in order to not do major damage to this guy. The entire time my heart is beating so loudly that I can feel it in my own throat. The man struggles against me for a few seconds before, eventually, he passes out.

Whew! Thank goodness. That was probably one of the scariest things I've ever done. I push the guy off me and drag him through the bars of a jail cell using my abilities. I grab a dusty sheet from the metal bed in the cell and tear it up. I tie a gag around his mouth and then bind his hands and feet, leaving him unconscious in the corner. I go back and get his gun. I use my strength to bend the muzzle so that the gun is no longer usable, and place it in his newly acquired jail cell.

I head back out in the hallway and stop prior to the corner that the guard had come from. I listen for any sounds of more guards. After a few seconds I feel confident the coast is clear and step into the hallway.

This one looks a little different; stark white walls with glass windows dotting the hallways, ending with a pair of windowless steel doors. I move to the first window and peer in carefully. An unconscious person lies on an exam table with tubes in their arms. A surgical tray with unidentified tools is at their side. I want to go help them but I can't chance waking someone up here. That would be another person I would have to carry with me; I can't risk that. I have to find my parents and Tony.

I continue down the hallway checking each window. Every time I hope that I'm going to find my parents or Tony, but no such luck so far. At the ninth window, I begin to feel like this mission may be hopeless. I peer in and find that this room is larger than the others are. A hospital curtain is drawn halfway around a table. I can only see the prisoner's feet.

Not wanting to leave any stone unturned, I step into the room to get a better look. That's when I see him. Even though his back is to me, I immediately recognize his hair and his tall, muscular frame. My heart starts racing. Not knowing what new abilities Zack may have acquired, I duck behind a small filing cabinet.

Zack opens the curtain a little further and looks around the room. I cringe and scoot further behind the cabinet. It isn't the best form of protection but it's something. I don't know if I can take Zack and I don't want to chance anything. Not with the red I saw in his eyes the last time we met. Plus, I have no idea what in the world he has turned into. Last I saw him in the mountain he only had one gift. It's obvious he's been experimenting with the immunizations. He may even be able to see through gifts now, which is why I hide in fear.

I hold my breath and make myself one with the cabinet as I hear the curtain open up further. I can't see what's going on but I hear a few footsteps and then the cling of instruments hitting the metal tray.

I wait for a few seconds before I get the courage to peak around the cabinet. When I do, my heart drops. I watch in horror as Zack finishes injecting the prisoner with a shot. Not just any shot, but a red shot. I can't see the prisoner because Zack is blocking him from my view.

I have to shrink back behind the cabinet when he starts to turn around. I listen to the sound of the needle hitting the tray and then the curtain is moved some more. More footsteps follow and then Zack comes into view.

My heart pounds in my chest and I swear he can hear it. He doesn't flinch though. Instead, he moves purposefully to the door and leaves the room.

In one strong whoosh, I release the breath I was holding. My stomach turns upside down as I quietly stand up. Whoever was given that red shot is either about to die or will be turning into a Reaper. Either way, it's a death sentence. I move hesitantly towards the curtain that Zack had fully closed.

At first, thoughts of a Reaper jumping out at me cross my mind. Then I remember when Tony told me about Chris, one of the soldiers who hated me, and his girlfriend who took the red shot. He said it took several days for her to turn after taking it.

I move a little more confidently to the curtain now. I grab the light blue fabric and begin pulling it back. When the prisoner comes into view, my knees buckle and I hit the floor. As if a freight train hit me straight in the chest, I suck in a haggard breath. Tears come to my eyes as I look up at Tony. "No!" I cry out in a muffled whisper. My heart beats heavily as I gain the energy to stand up and move to his side.

He too has a patch on his arm and he's unconscious but breathing. I reach out and run my hand through his copper hair. He looks so peaceful. He has no idea what was injected into his blood stream. He doesn't know that in a few days he will turn into the very monster he worked so hard to destroy.

I don't realize I'm crying until my tears land on his arm. This can't be happening! He cannot turn into a Reaper! My hands ball up as I consider the complete unfairness of this situation. He saved me. I was supposed to save him! He doesn't deserve this fate! No, I can't deal with this. I just realized that I may have feelings for this man and now he's going to die? No!

I kick the wall next to the examination table, leaving a heavy indentation in the paint. "Crap!" I cry out. That freaking hurt! I have to walk around in a few small circles to walk off the pain, praying all the while that no one heard that. If I have any chance of getting Tony out of here, he has to be awake.

This sobers me up. "Screw this!" I yank the patch off his arm and place my hand right over his heart. Maybe I can heal him. Perhaps if I try hard enough, I can heal whatever that red shot is doing to his body. I focus all of my energy on helping him.

Within a few seconds, he opens his eyes. He looks up at me as if in a dream. Realization plays across his expression and then he darts up off the bed lightning fast. He moves so quickly that I start to fall back. Life feels like it is going in slow motion as my weary body falls backwards.

He catches me before I hit the ground and pulls me to him. "Willow." He strokes my hair; my face is planted in his chest. I feel so tired but I still notice how good he smells. Like fresh cut grass and soap. "Willow, you have to open your eyes. You can't pass out now," he whispers in my ear.

The darkness is calling my name. He shakes me some more. "Not right now. Focus on healing. You can do it. Heal yourself. I believe in you. I need you."

With his words of encouragement, I focus on healing once again. This time I focus my abilities inwardly. I begin feeling more alert in less than a minute. My muscles strengthen up and, eventually, I find the ability to stand on my own.

Begrudgingly I back away just enough to look into his eyes. They are still the same beautiful neon yellow they have always been. My heart catches as I realize how close we are. "Hi," I whisper in a throaty voice.

His eyes light up and he smiles slightly. "Hi." Time stops in that moment as we stare into each other's eyes. He breaks the silence that's settled over us by saying, "You saved me."

I nod my head.

"Thank you." He runs his hand through my hair.

I hold my breath. What an awkward situation for such a beautiful moment to occur. His hand moves to my cheek and I rest my head into it.

"You're welcome," I say.

He slowly drops his hand to his side. My cheek still feels warm from his touch. "We need to get out of here, Willow. They're planning some crazy stuff."

I nod my head. "Yes, we have a team inside right now doing reconnaissance. We have to find my parents first though."

"Definitely," he says. His face turns serious for a moment. "I don't want to alarm you but I have to tell you that I haven't seen your parents; not since we saw them taken down in that field. I did my best to look around the room they herded us into at the beginning, but didn't have any luck."

A lump forms in my throat as my brain starts pondering a million things a minute. "Do you think they survived? Why wouldn't they be in here?"

He places his hand in mine and gives it a small squeeze. I rub my thumb over the side of his hand, trying to squelch the feelings I'm having. "Don't worry, Willow. I'm sure they're fine. The room was huge and filled with chaos. It's very possible that I didn't see them."

I doubt that. Tony is very observant and I'm sure he could spot my mom from a mile away. He was trained to look after his leader. "I hope so." A thought comes to mind. "Do you think they got away? Perhaps before they brought everyone here?" I say as false hope fills me.

His expression tells me that he highly doubts that possibility but he humors me anyway. "You never know. Anything could have happened."

My eyes widen at the thought of 'anything' since that's such a broad range of outcomes; including horrible ones.

He sees my thought process and quickly adds, "I mean, yes, they could have gotten away. They could be safe and sound this very second."

"But you don't think so," I say, hoping I'm wrong.

His expression softens. "I think that your mom is a very strong woman. Your dad has to be one heck of a guy too, in order to keep up with her. I think they'll survive. We do need to find them quickly though. I don't know what Dr. Hastings's plans are, but they can't be good. Not with how that militia swooped in like that, shooting people point blank. I don't care if they were tranquilizers or not. That was definitely a hostile takeover."

"Yes it was." The memory of the scene sends chills up my spine. Dr. Hastings's plans can't be good, especially not if his son Zack was shooting Tony up with the kill shot. My chest tightens. I can't let Tony become a Reaper. I can't think about that right now though. I focus my mind knowing I need my thoughts to be clear. My parent's lives are on the line.

"We should get a move on," Tony says.

"Okay." I grab my backpack that I had set on the floor and hand Tony my extra pistol with some ammo. He gladly accepts and puts the gun under his shirt at the small of his back. Hot! Urgh, when did I start thinking about Tony this way? I don't know. All I know is that now, this man next to me makes my palms sweat and my stomach flutter. This is such horrible timing to be developing these feelings.

"Ready?" He holds his hand out for me to accept.

I wipe mine off on my jeans, nod, and then take his hand. He smiles and squeezes my fingers gently. With Tony's hand in mine we head out of the room and move into the hallway, careful not to run into anyone.

Thankfully, we don't notice any signs of guards in the vicinity. We make our way up the row of windows checking each one carefully. I can tell that Tony wants so badly to help the other prisoners, as do I. There will have to be another time for that though.

After checking the last room at the end of the hall next to the steel doors, we realize that my parents aren't in this area.

"We need to go in there," Tony says quietly, while pointing towards the steel doors.

"Do you know what's on the other side?" I ask, hoping he may have some inside knowledge.

"No, this hall is as far as they took me." His expression turns serious.

"Well, I guess it looks like we are going in blind." I reposition my hand in his. "Hopefully anyone on the other side is blind too, at least when it comes to seeing powers." I turn us invisible again.

The steel doors don't seem to be locked but I use

my gift to move us through the doors anyway. After all, if a door magically opens, I doubt that someone on the other side would blame it on a ghost.

We step through to the other side effortlessly and find ourselves in the middle of a large room that I assume is either a clinic or the prison hospital. A few makeshift hallways run behind rows and rows of curtains that are all attached to tracks on the ceiling. The smell of ammonia burns my nose and I find myself having to breathe through my mouth. A fluorescent light in the corner of the giant room is on its last leg, so it's flickering eerily.

A sinking feeling starts welling up in the pit of my stomach. Everything about this place tells me to run. There isn't a soul in sight and the room is so silent that all I can hear is Tony's and my breathing.

Tony gently squeezes my hand. I look up at him and find comfort in knowing that he's just as thoroughly freaked out as I am.

We walk silently down the corridor of curtains, peeking into each one as we go. Nobody occupies them, so we continue moving. When we peek into the fifth curtain, I suddenly remember why I hate odd numbers so much. I double over and dry heave from the sight. If I had any food in my stomach, I would have spilled it onto the floor. The poignant copper scent fills my nose and throat, causing me to gag even more. Tony pulls me to him and tries rubbing my back in comfort. Eventually the dry heaving calms enough for me to stand back up. This room is covered in so much blood that it's impossible for me to fathom where it all came from. It stains the white linen coverings of the bed. The floor is wet and sticky from it and the rear curtain has splatters of red across it.

"What happened here?" Tony asks. I look at him since this is the last place we should be talking and realize I must be reading his mind.

"I have no idea, but we have to find my parents. Now!" I think to myself.

"I agree!" Tony confirms.

I look up at him in utter confusion. "Did I just say that last sentence out loud? I know I thought it. This is freaky."

"I can hear you, Willow. In my head." Tony looks at me in wonder.

"Weird... No time to contemplate it though, we have to find my parents," I tell him telepathically. Man, this is just too convenient that this would happen now of all times. Now the risk for being heard talking is nil.

"Yes, let's get out of this place." He takes my hand and pulls me away from the nightmarish scene. My stomach continues to twist in knots and it's extremely difficult for me to push the visual of that room from my mind. I do my best though. I have to focus. "Should we try the door up ahead or should we pick a wall and walk through it?" I have no idea where my parents would be kept in this place.

"Let's stick with the doors for now," he thinks, and I nod in acknowledgement.

We both move quickly to the end of the room, desperately wanting to leave this horrible area. I focus my powers and walk us through the doors and into a short, empty hallway. No windows or cells dot this hallway. Within a few steps, we are at a new set of doors. This one looks like it has a type of keycard access panel that's lit with a red dot.

Ignoring the security measures they put in place, I walk Tony through the reinforced doors. My back goes rigid, my muscles tense and Tony pulls me to the side, behind a pair of fake Ficus trees.

This area is not empty. Not at all! There are dozens of guards coming to and from what I assume is a command center. Cubicles are set up in geometric patterns with computer workstations at each one. There are women and men sitting behind most of the computers. We stay silent and hide behind the little cover the trees offer. I just hope that nobody possesses the gift to see us.

We wait a few minutes, observing all that's going on. I watch the workers and the guards who are dressed in matching black uniforms, hustling here and there. Every once in a while a few people in blue surgical scrubs come and go from what I assume is a break room. I look around trying to best assess our plan of action, as does Tony.

A man in scrubs approaches in our direction. I lean into Tony on impulse and he puts his arm around me. I hold my breath when the man gets close enough to see us. Seeing he has navy eyes, I let out a breath. He passes us without notice and opens a door in the corner of the room. Before he steps into the room, I catch a glimpse of several racks filled with surgical equipment and scrubs. I can tell that Tony takes notice of it too.

"Are you thinking what I'm thinking?" I ask Tony.

"You tell me. You're the one listening to my mind," he jokes.

"Funny." I look up at him and roll my eyes. "I'm thinking we may not be this lucky next time."

"True. We better go incognito then."

I nod my head.

We wait for the guy to exit the small supply closet. Once he's far enough away, we make our move. I pull Tony into the closet. We look around at the medical supplies, scanning the shelves. There are several sets of surgical scrubs stacked on the top shelf. We both grab a pair at least one size bigger than we usually wear to fit over our clothes. We put them on as quickly as possible.

"You ready?" he asks me.

"Yes." I say. I let go of our invisibility and do something I haven't done in a while: I reach for the doorknob. We exit the closet with the greatest of care to not draw attention to ourselves. Without the veil of invisibility, it makes me feel completely vulnerable. Thankfully, nobody even acknowledges our presence. We walk through the main room, taking time to peek in when we reach the break area. We both try to keep our eyes focused downward. I feel naked and exposed out in the open like this.

Suddenly alarms are blaring and strobe lights are flashing. "What the heck did we do?"

"I don't think we did anything," he says, trying not to panic.

All the people around us stop what they're doing and begin running in the same direction. A guard yells out above the chaos, "Code Orange."

I glance at Tony momentarily and hear him say, "Just run with them." I nod my head and we're off. We follow the masses of people out into the courtyard that runs along the fence line towards the front gates. I immediately get nervous as the guards with guns begin pointing them in our general direction.

We watch as all the people from inside form a barrier at the gates. Tony and I quickly line up alongside them, trying desperately to play the part.

The alarms and strobe lights die off almost instantaneously and everyone around us stands stoically, not moving a muscle. Facing forward, eyes never wavering. The doors we came through open one last time and my stomach drops. Zack and Dr. Hastings emerge carrying massive assault rifles. I swallow the lump that's formed in my throat. They come to the middle of the courtyard and wait... for what I'm not sure. The doors behind them open once more and four people emerge. Two of them are bound together with steel chains and black cloth sacks have been pulled over their heads, making them indistinguishable. The other two guards have them by the crook of their arm, ushering them to where Zack and Dr. Hastings stand.

They each grab one of the black sacks and simultaneously pull them off the prisoner's heads. My knees threaten to buckle when I stare back at my mother and father.

My dad shakes his hair out of his eyes. My mother doesn't have to shake her hair back because Zack does it for her. His face so sinister and menacing… it makes me want to risk everything to run to them. Tony holds me back though. "Not yet."

Zack puts his hand under my mother's chin, lifting it up for inspection. My dad tries to yell between his gag to stop him but it only comes out as a jumble of grunts. My mother turns her face quickly to the left, releasing herself from Zack's grip.

Dr. Hastings then turns toward us 'onlookers' and addresses us. "As you all know, we are under a code orange. This means we detected infiltration from the outside and went into lock down mode. All those with the gift of purple have been sent into the fields around us to pick out the intruders as they attempt to escape. Since I know they haven't all left, one in particular, we've decided to provide some entertainment. Willow…"

I hear my name and it sends ice through my veins. It ricochets off the walls a few times and Tony's grip tightens tenfold on my hand. "Don't do anything irrational, Willow. We have to wait if we're going to win this game."

I can't answer him now. Not even in my head. My parents are in harm's way and the outcome can't be good. I try to use my gift to see what the future holds but I am too shaken up to make it work.

"Willow," Dr. Hastings continues. "I have something you want, and you have something I want. I know you're here… I can feel it." He stops talking for a moment, letting what he says seep in.

One of the guards brings a briefcase and places it at Dr. Hastings's feet. Dr. Hastings bends down and unlatches it, pulling out a long syringe with a clear liquid. He flicks it with his finger and pushes the syringe up just enough so that a small amount sprays from the top.

My heart is beating with the pulse of a thousand horses. My breathing grows ragged as tears come to my eyes. I don't look away though, no, I can't give up my position now. I may be the only one who can save my parents at this point. Dr. Hastings comes around to the back of my mother and places his free hand on her shoulder; taking the time to place his fingers down one at a time. I can see my mother trying to move but it's no use. The straps that have her tied down are just too strong.

"All I need is a pint of your blood, Willow," Dr. Hastings says while running the needle around the surface of my mother's neck. "Just one pint," he reiterates. I struggle to hold on to my sensibility instead of running immediately to my mother's aid. Tony's right. If I have any chance of winning this evil game Dr. Hastings has created, patience is my greatest ally.

"However, if you don't want to give it to me, then I'll take the one thing you love most from this world." Dr. Hastings takes his hand from my mother's shoulder and pulls her face to the side, exposing her neck even more. I swallow the bowling ball that's lodged in my throat. My hands are shaking in anticipation. I'm fearful that I may not know the difference between the right time, and the point of no return.

"Steady," Tony's whisper enters my thoughts.

"I bet you're wondering what's in the shot," Zack says, pointing to the syringe in his father's hands. "That is a mega dose of the stuff they use for lethal injections. It will kill your mother the instant it reaches her blood," he says nonchalantly, smiling back at the crowd of onlookers.

Behind the gate, I hear a few shouts… one sounds like Mr. Leroy, but I can't be sure. I just really hope they're all going to be okay.

"This is your last chance, Willow, your last chance," Dr. Hastings says once more.

I'm screaming inside for Tony to do something, anything! A timer flashes on the side of the building being lit from an unknown source. It has thirty seconds lit up on it. Then it begins to tick down: twenty-nine, twenty-eight. I try reasoning with Tony, begging him to help me do something, anything! The clock is at fifteen seconds and I'm about to come unglued.

"A pint of my blood or my mother's life," I repeat over and over in my head. Is this really a choice I need to make? It seems so simple.

Tony comes through my thoughts. "No! Dr. Hastings would never take just a pint of blood. He will kill you. I swore to your mom that I would protect you at all costs. Your mother wouldn't want you to sacrifice yourself. If she had the ability, she wouldn't let you."

I fight back, yelling in my head. "I can't just watch my mother die!" I grit my teeth, biting my tongue to keep from shouting.

Ten, nine… The anxiety is so intense that I find myself paralyzed by it. A single tear slips down my cheek as I frantically look at Dr. Hastings, Zack, the needle, my mother… I open my mouth to call out, not able to take it any longer. But then I hear a popping sound; like something coming apart that was never meant to do so. I watch as my mother frees up her left hand from one of the ties. Hope builds in me as I expect her to break free. That's why it takes me a second to process what happens next. As if in slow motion, I watch her hand reach upward. She swiftly removes the syringe from Dr. Hastings's grip and plunges it into her neck. I stare in horror as she injects herself with the drug. As if in slow motion, she falls slowly to her knees and then face down on the ground. Her life force ripped from her in an instant.

"No!!!" I yell, expecting people to turn in my direction, but I must be crying out in my mind. I reach my hand out and my knees buckle beneath me, but Tony pulls me close to his side preventing me from falling. "No…" I whimper aloud quietly. "I can help her!" I tell Tony.

"No, Willow. She's gone. She did that for you. You have to stay strong. Please stand back up," he urges me.

Before I can process what's happening, chaos from the crowd of people erupts and they begin to rush Zack and Dr. Hastings. I hear some of their thoughts like, "that was our only hope", and, "what are we supposed to do now?"

I feel like a rag doll when Tony pulls me with him. "Get us through the bars, Willow, now!"

I look him in the eyes. It's like he's speaking another language. I can't understand what he's saying.

"We have to go!" he yells out loud.

I shake my head. "My dad. My mom." Something breaks inside me with the last two words.

He sets me down on the ground and I watch, with a glazed expression, people running around panicking, trying to figure out what to do.

I didn't even notice Tony leave until he returns with my dad at his side. My father's arms and legs are free and he looks just as broken as I do. His eyes are glazed over as if he still can't process what just happened.

I hear something that sounds as if it could be the bars behind me bending. The next thing I know, Mr. Leroy is running past us into the mix of chaos. He returns a second later with my mother's lifeless body in his arms. That's when my father's knees hit the ground. He puts his hands over his face and falls face forward to the earth, sobbing heavily.

I should comfort him but I can't move. I can't take my eyes off my mother's small and ever so still form. Tony puts his hand on my back. With that, my breath catches, my heart breaks and the flood gates open. Tears that I can't control stream down my face like a river of sorrow. I reach out to heal my mother, but Tony stops my hands. I try to break free to do something, anything, to help my mother. "She's gone," Tony keeps whispering over and over again in my ear.

A man and woman with yellow eyes, whom I barely

know, come to my father's side. They each grab one of my father's arms, lifting him up between them, and begin running towards the trees.

Lee follows them, holding my mother, and Tony whisks me into his arms. We fit perfectly through the bars and our group takes off running at full speed away from the prison walls.

I don't recall the trip back to the safe house. I find myself too drained to do anything but lie limp in Tony's arms. I can't even cry anymore. My face is tucked into his chest so he can't see me. I refuse to open my eyes or say anything even when Tony persistently asks me if I'm okay. He tries to ask me through his thoughts, so I close myself off to that ability somehow.

I feel as if I have ceased to exist. That this world has brought nothing but pain to me and at this point I'm done with it. I don't have to talk, move, or open my eyes ever again. Just like my mom... My chest aches with the thought. I hate feeling! If only I could turn it off.

I assume by the people's cries that we've arrived back at the safe house. I know that not only my mom is being brought home to rest, but several other soldiers as well. I heard the whispers as we ran. The guards had attacked a group on the other side of the prison. They barely made it out alive.

I don't want to witness any of this so I tuck my head further into Tony's chest, trying desperately to block it out. We are still outside and I can hear as the others run up to our party sobbing and calling out cries to Heaven. The wails rip and thrash at my soul like hungry hands trying to tear the last part of me down. I can't take it anymore. I tell him, "Take me inside."

He squeezes me gently as he lets out a sigh of relief after finally hearing that I'm not comatose. "Of course." He starts walking again; this time, thankfully, away from the crowd.

"No!!!" I hear a high-pitched cry and the sound of feet running in our direction.

"Willow!" I flinch at the sound of my name being called by Alec, and possibly Claire, from afar.

They reach us in a second. I know I need to turn around and tell my friends that I'm not dead. I can only guess that was their assumption since Tony is carrying me. I just feel like I can't face them. Like I can't open my eyes and see them, because, if I do, everything will be real. My mother's death will be real. I can't take this pain; it hurts too much.

"She's alive," Tony says quickly as they approach.

Claire lets out a loud sob of relief.

"She's alive; she's going to be okay." Connor comforts his girlfriend.

"Is she hurt? Tell me what happened!" Alec demands with a forceful voice.

"Physically, no... Mentally, more than we can comprehend. She just watched her mother sacrifice herself to save her." Tony doesn't seem too thrilled by Alec's presence either.

"Alice is dead?" Claire asks bluntly.

I can feel Tony nodding his head and he pulls me closer to him. "You can comfort her," he says to Alec. "He can help you." With that, he gently pulls me from his chest and tries to move me into Alec's arms.

"No." I cling to Tony's shirt.

"I don't think I'm the one she needs right now. We broke up today." There is a slight mix of bitterness with a hint of pain in his voice.

"Oh." Tony says. "You didn't tell me." He says it in more of a statement than a question.

I don't answer. I just grip his shirt tighter. "Please, just take me inside."

"She wants to go inside," Tony tells them.

"Do you want me to come with you?" Claire asks.

"Please tell her I can't right now," I tell Tony. I just want to curl up into a ball and let the world pass away before my eyes. I don't want conversation or comfort. I just want my mom.

"I think she just wants to be alone right now," Tony tells her.

"Okay," Claire says hesitantly. "We love you, Willow. All of us do. We're here for you when you're ready." I feel her hand's warmth on my back.

"Thank you," Tony tells them.

He starts moving again, using his foot to push the door open. He carries me up a few flights of stairs and opens another door. He closes it behind him and then gently places me on the bed.

Instinctively, I curl into myself in the fetal position.

"I'll let you rest, Willow. I'll be right outside if you need me. Just call for me." He brushes my hair back.

I don't open my eyes when I say internally, "Please don't leave me." It's the only cry for help I can manage right now.

"Never." He takes off my shoes. He then takes off his and lies down in the bed behind me, pulling me into him. He holds me tight against his chest. "I'm here. You can let it out now."

With that, the tears let loose again. I allow them to fall. He strokes my hair and holds me tight. He doesn't tell me that it will be okay or that she's in a better place. He just lets me mourn.

I grip Tony's shirt and ball it into my fists. I feel like if I let him go my world will completely fall apart. My mother... the woman I used to call mommy, is no longer here. Choking sobs bellow from my mouth as I try to get my mind to understand what has happened.

I have flashbacks of all the beautiful memories of my mother and me. Her pushing me on the swing, her laughing as the top of the blender comes off, leaving a ginormous mess in the kitchen. I remember her stroking my hair at bedtime and always being there to tuck me in. I remember sitting in her lap as she would read me story after story telling me that someday my prince would come.

Then something dawns on me... Sebastian! What on earth are we going to tell my baby brother? Is he old enough to understand? The idea of him falling apart makes me grip Tony's shirt even tighter... like the security blanket

I used to own. I don't think I've ever felt this much grief in my life... and I hope I never will again. Not even when we had to leave my mother and Sebastian at the mountain. At least then, I held onto the hope that they were going to be okay. That they were going to make it.

That night I end up falling into a dark and dreamless sleep, holding onto Tony for dear life.

Nothingness. That's what I feel right now.

I guess it's better than anything else is on a day like today.

Claire brought me up a long black dress. She stands behind me, twisting my hair into a bun. She places tiny pieces of baby's breath she found in the garden sporadically through my hair. I don't recognize the person staring back at me... that person who looks so haunted. My eyes have become shrunken and hollow, my skin looks pasty white. It's obvious that my body is lacking in sustenance. I haven't eaten since who knows when.

It was only yesterday that my mother died. Out here, they bury the bodies quick. They buried the rest of the lost ones last night and waited till the morning for my mom. You can feel the tension that lies in the air from all the people who have lost their leader.

I look through my peripheral vision at my little brother lying on my bed. I stifle a sob as I remember my dad and me telling Sebastian what happened early this morning. My memory of it is fresh and I can still see his cherub cheeks stained with tears. His little eyes turned bloodshot. His curls stuck to his forehead. He dropped to the floor and screamed if anyone tried to touch him. He exhausted himself so much that he fell asleep in the bed next to me, clenching my mother's old sweater. Even now, dried tears cling to his face and every now and then, he whimpers "Mommy," in his sleep.

Claire places the last clip in my hair and gives my arms a tender touch. "Thank you Claire," I manage to say, although my voice is noticeably hoarse.

"Not a problem," she replies back to me. Claire looks down at her watch. "We only have a few more minutes. It's probably time to head downstairs."

I give her a slight nod and stand to my feet. I pick up Sebastian gently in my arms. His little eyes flutter open and he asks for mommy. I purse my lips and shake my head. "Mommy's gone, baby. Mommy's gone." His eyes squeeze shut and his face curls up into me, similar to how I did to Tony last night.

We get to the bottom of the staircase and see everyone gathering in the old ballroom. Someone must have taken the time to tune the grand piano because there is soft music playing. Amazing Grace, I know that one.

Claire must sense my hesitation because she places her hand around my middle. "It'll be okay. We'll get through this together."

I take a deep breath, steadying myself before I enter the room. All eyes turn to me as I walk in. It's almost too much and I consider walking out, but Claire's hand remains strong around me, helping me to the front.

I get nauseous as I notice my mother's handmade coffin positioned just a few feet from me. The lid is down, thankfully. Tony and three other soldiers stand two by two at each side of the coffin, as if to either protect my mom or to stand by her side for the final time.

"Are you okay?" His face looks worried and I can tell he's torn about wanting to be with me at this time. I nod my head gently and take a seat.

My father comes to sit next to me. He looks about as bad as I do, if not worse. He doesn't smile in my presence; he just squeezes my hand and kisses Sabby's curls.

Mr. Leroy comes to the front of the room with a Bible and a few notecards in his hand. He places them on a podium and clears his throat.

"I wish I was standing before you under different circumstances. Today we honor the life of one of our most cherished soldiers… Alice Rose Mosby."

I take a moment to look at the casket before me. Several kinds of delicate flowers line the coffin, giving it a comforting feeling. I look back up to Mr. Leroy as he continues, "Alice was an amazing woman. She had a heart of gold. She was a devoted mother and wife, and a great leader. Today our hearts mourn for the loss of someone so special… our hearts ache." Mr. Leroy clears his throat. You can see the tears in his eyes and the fact that he is trying to get through this, one moment at a time.

I lay my head on Claire's shoulder and close my eyes. I could listen to her eulogy, or I could close my eyes and transport myself back to the beautiful memories I hold of my mother. Sabby twitches a little in my arms but falls back to sleep. I think of my mother: her smile, her laugh, her quirky antics. I remember how amazing she was and what a not so good cook she was. Every time she would try to make dinner, she would burn it. One time she used salt instead of sugar in a pie recipe. She was so excited she hadn't burnt it until we took our first bite. We laughed and teased her about it long after the evening was over. She would never live that down. I replay these memories over and over again in my head, never wanting to forget.

I'm brought back to the present when Claire's shoulder lifts, making my head go up with it. I glance over at her and she points to the coffin. Mr. Leroy has finished his speech and there is not a dry eye in the crowd. I watch as Mr. Leroy comes and stands by the coffin. "For those of you that desire closure we will be opening the casket one last time before burial. Please allow the family some privacy and then form a line." Tony and another soldier gently lift the lid, placing it next to the coffin against the wall.

My breath hitches as I see my mother lying lifeless before me. She looks so beautiful. She's been dressed in a lovely, yet simple, ivory dress. Her hair and makeup are done as well. She holds a bouquet of purple flowers in her hands, which have been placed over her heart. My brain wants to convince me that she's only sleeping. That she can't look this beautiful and really be dead. I realize I need to wake Sabby. He can't miss these final bittersweet moments with his mom.

I gently wake him up and a tear escapes his eye

when he sees it's me and not mom waking him. I sit him up, making him look at me. "Sabby, it's time to say goodbye." I want to say more to him, but I can't think of what to say. So I take his hand and, together with my dad, we walk up to the open casket.

Sebastian doesn't waste a second reaching in to touch her cold skin. "Mommy." He gives her a small shake as if he's trying to wake her from a deep sleep.

"Sabby," I say, while bending down to his level. "It may look like she's sleeping but really she's not there. Her soul has left and is with the angels now."

His brown eyes stare up at me and his brows crinkle. "She's wite here, Wello!" he demands. Tears begin to fall freely and I see he won't understand. Not now... not till he's older. I take him into my arms and watch as my father leans over and gives my mother's lips a light kiss. He takes something out of his pocket and places it into her casket. It's a very small stuffed animal that looks as if it's seen better days. I remember the story behind it. It was the item my father gave to my mother on their first date at a carnival. He had tried to win her the big prize but ended up spending way too much money earning her only the little prize. She didn't mind though. She always loved what it symbolized. I'm surprised she had found a way to keep it through everything that was going on.

My dad takes Sebastian from my arms. "Take your time," he says to me.

I nod my head, not sure what to do. I stand alone, next to my mother's lifeless body. I take her hand in mine and rub it like she used to do with me when I was little. "Mommy," I say through the tears. I can't get much out before I lose it, falling to my knees next to her casket. "Mommy, I'm so sorry. I'm so sorry." The guilt and blame are eating me alive and I feel like this is all my fault. I feel like I killed her and it's killing me inside.

I don't know how long I stay kneeled by her casket, holding my mother's hand. The next thing I remember is Claire coming to my side and helping me to my feet. Her cheeks are stained with tears as well. "Claire," I confess. "I don't know how to let go." I look down at my mother's hand in mine. "If I let her go, I'll never see her again." I begin to panic, my breathing increases.

"Willow," Claire reasons. "You will see her again someday. Just not in this lifetime. She's looking down from above admiring what an amazing legacy she left behind. She wouldn't want you to cry like this for her. She would want you say goodbye, to remember all the good times and the fun times you shared together. She would want you to help your father and little brother. She once told me you were the strong one... the glue to the family."

I look in Claire's eyes. "She said that?" I ask her.

She nods her head. "Yes, and she meant it."

I bite my lip knowing that time is drawing this to an end. I take a flower from the bouquet she's holding and clutch it in my hand. "I'm going to dry this so I'll always remember her sacrifice and what she did for me... for all of us." I take one last look at my mother and turn my back. Realizing it's not forever makes me feel a little better.

Tony and the other soldiers are the pallbearers. Someone plays a beautiful melody on the violin as we follow my mother's casket outside. Near the trees, we stop around a small hole made in the dirt. I hold on tight to my father and my brother's hands as we watch them slowly lower my mother into the ground.

Alec and Connor stand to the side with shovels in their hands. I hadn't seen them inside the hotel earlier. I hadn't seen much of anything, though, through the tears and the pain. When it's their turn, they slowly shovel dirt one by one into the hole.

Part way through, Mr. Leroy taps on Connor's shoulder and requests that he have a turn. He shovels a scoop of dirt into the hole and then hands his shovel to another person waiting behind him.

Realizing that this is some sort of closure type ritual, Alec hands his shovel to Tony. Afterwards, Alec makes eye contact with me. I mouth, "thank you," to him and he nods his head graciously.

Tony drops a pile of dirt in and then brings the shovel to my father. My father accepts it and walks dutifully towards my mother's grave. I know it takes everything within him to cover her casket with one more layer of dirt, but he does it. Sebastian and I walk to his side. Instead of using the shovel, Sebastian leans over and scoops up a handful of dirt. He holds his little hand over the hole and lets the dirt fall slowly. It takes everything in me not to completely lose it. Someone hands me the second shovel and I gather earth into it and drop it in. Then we hand our shovels to the others who have lined up to pay their respects in this way.

After the final layer of dirt has covered my mother's grave, we each drop wildflowers on it. By the time it's my turn to lie a dandelion down, my mother's grave has become a masterpiece of beautiful colors. I close my eyes and let the flower fall. Dandelions always were her favorite.

Mr. Leroy leads us in a prayer at the end and then we retreat inside. I didn't notice until I started walking towards the hotel that there are seven other graves surrounding my mother's. She will not be alone. I walk with my family and my friends inside where a meal has been prepared for us.

For the most part, we eat in silence. I don't have an appetite though, even if I can't remember the last time I ate. I move my food around my plate, concentrating on this simple action instead of inviting hoards of unpleasant thoughts to run through my head. I watch my dad and Sabby do the same.

"You need to eat," Tony speaks to my thoughts from across the room.

I look up from my pitiful plate and shake my head. "I can't," I say back to him mindlessly. I don't feel like even sitting here right now. I tell my dad that I'm going to go and lie down. Leaving my plate on the table, I head upstairs.

I can feel Tony's presence before I can even hear him. I can't explain why all of a sudden I feel so connected to him. It's as if something happened when we were at the prison. Ever since then I can tell when he's around, not to mention the fact that I can speak to him with my mind.

I wonder why I can't do this with anyone else? The only thing I can think of is it may have to do with Zack and his experimentations.

I feel Tony's arm reach around my middle and rest on my hip. Without thinking, I lean into his shoulder, letting him carry a portion of my body weight. Sometimes I guess it just feels better to know that you have someone to help you when you can't even help yourself.

Tony follows me to my room and closes the door behind him. In any other situation, this would make butterflies dance in my stomach, but not today. Today I just need to exist. I climb under the covers and curl into myself. Tony, like the gentleman he is, remains on top of the covers and puts his arms around me. He squeezes gently but enough to make me feel grounded, like I am still an inhabitant on this earth.

I turn around to face Tony. His hair has grown out a lot in the last few weeks. I reach up and brush it out of his eyes. His yellow eyes stare back at me… except there is a red speck in them. I'm sure it wasn't there before. Panic begins to rise in my chest and without thinking; I begin to heal Tony through my touch. I'm not sure if it'll work or not, but it's worth a try. I hold Tony's gaze and a few moments later the spec has dematerialized.

I watch as Tony's eyebrows crease in the middle. "Why are your eyes blue?" he asks me aloud. He brushes my long bangs from my face, taking in my eyes.

"Oh," I say, realizing I can't tell him the true reason. "You had a scratch on your face. It must have been from yesterday. I was just taking care of it for you." I bite my lip instinctively, hoping he won't catch the deceit in my voice. Much to my relief, he simply smiles back and tells me thank you.

I curl up into his chest and he wraps his arms fully around me. I can't help but feel safe in his arms. As if nothing in this world could ever hurt me. If only I could just stay like this forever.

Thoughts of last night begin invading my mind. Visions of Tony being injected by that red shot, plays itself over and over again in my head. I try to squelch the panic but I'm having a hard time. It wells up inside me and tries it's best to choke me. I feel like everyone I love is going to be taken from me! I hope with all I am that I can keep Tony from turning into a Reaper... but what if I can't? Do I tell him? No, I can't. It wouldn't be fair for him to lose the last few days he has if I can't stop this.

I clench my fists unknowingly. My heart starts accelerating and I can feel my cheeks heating up. None of this is fair! I breathe out a long, shaky breath.

"Are you okay?" Tony asks concerned.

I give out a shaky, "Yes."

He tries to stare me down, knowing full well that I'm not sharing what I'm really feeling. Not wanting to talk about it, I turn over.

He pulls me closer so that my back is against his chest. "I know it's hard, Willow. If you need to cry some more, I'm not going to tell you not to."

I don't answer him. I don't need to cry. No, the

emotions that I'm feeling are not just grief. No, this is much stronger and thicker than grief; this is anger. This isn't fair! None of it! My mom is gone and in a few days, I could very well be losing Tony. I pull a spare pillow up to my chest, clenching both corners of it with my hands. Needing to let my feelings out physically, I alternate between twisting it and gripping it tightly like a stress ball.

My blood starts pumping through my veins more rapidly. How did everything go down like this so quickly? How did my life get flipped on its axis in a matter of a day? You know the answer, Willow! I think to myself. My blood starts to boil. I know very well how my life got totally flipped up...the Hastings' men! My breath quickens and my pulse speeds up at the thought of the two people hell bent on making my life, and everyone else's, miserable, for their own personal, selfish gain. All of this, every single thing I am feeling right now, is because of them! My mom should not be dead! They killed her! Tony should not be turning into a Reaper! They caused it! They should be dead! They should... as the thought is spoken aloud in my mind, the plan starts formulating in my head. My heart is beating as quickly as the thoughts are coming, lighting fast. They will pay!

I hear the sound of something tearing. "Willow!" Tony sits up quickly.

I look down at the feathers my pillow has vomited up. My hands clench each corner of its torn cover.

Tony grabs my arm and pulls me over to face him. "Willow, you need to breathe. It's going to be okay.

Everything will be okay."

I dart up out of bed like a lightning bolt. "No, Tony! It will not be okay. It will never be okay!" I angrily point towards somewhere on the other side of the window. "They did this! They need to pay!" My breath starts catching and I feel my heart skip a beat before it starts pumping wildly. "I will make them pay! Right now!" A dizzy sensation washes over me and the world starts to tilt.

Tony's eyes widen in shock; he then darts up and forces me to sit in a nearby chair. He pushes my head down between my legs. "Breathe, Willow." He holds my back down and accentuates his breathing in and out in long, deep breaths. "You're having a panic attack."

Thoughts of the nurse outside the shelter come to me. I don't want to think of that day. I focus on breathing in and out.

Finally, the dizziness subsides and Tony allows me to sit back up. He quickly kneels in front of me and examines my eyes. Whatever he sees comes as a relief to him. He seems to ponder on something for a second before he relinquishes it. "Your eyes were red."

I lift my fingers up to my eyes in surprise. "What color are they now?" My chest feels tight with anxiety.

"Dark blue." He puts his hand on my knee. "You must have used your healing ability to stave off the panic attack. Whatever just happened a few minutes ago was caused by your anger. You have to find a way to control it, Willow, or it will control you."

I shake my head and this time tears come to my

75

eyes. "I have to hold onto the anger, Tony. Dr. Hastings and Zack deserve to pay for what they've done. I will make them pay if it's the last thing I do."

Tony stands up and starts pacing. "You can't just go after them like that, Willow."

I jump up out of the chair. "See, that's where you're wrong. I can and I will!"

He stops and stares me down. I don't back down or look away. Finally, he says, "I understand your need to avenge your mother. I feel the same way trust me, but we have to have a plan. You can't just dilly-dally in there and go all guns a blazing. They have a lot of manpower."

"Yeah well, I don't really care. I will go after them. Plus, a lot of that 'manpower' seemed to revolt there at the end for whatever reason."

Tony stops, remembering that last moment when everyone ran after the Hastings men. "You're right. They probably already killed them."

The thought makes me angry. "Either way, I'm going after them. I won't stop until I know they are dead."

"What is killing them going to do for you, Willow?" Exasperated, Tony runs his hand through his hair.

"Do you not realize what they've done? How much pain they've caused? They have killed people that I love! I won't let them take another life." I realize I'm adding Tony into the count of the people they've killed. The thought runs like ice through my veins. I start pacing, as if the steps can push reality away for a moment.

Tony doesn't notice the addition. His expression

softens. "If this is something you have to do, then I'll go with you."

I stop mid-step and look at him. I didn't doubt that he would stand at my side just like he did my mothers. I just didn't know there would be so much turmoil and worry for my well-being in the mix. I can tell just by his expression, and the feelings emanating off him in palpable waves, that he cares about my welfare a lot more than a friend would. He is deathly scared of losing me. He steps forward, places one of his hands on my hip, and uses the other to push a stray strand of hair behind my ear.

My heart rate accelerates again, but this time it's accompanied by a fluttering sensation in my stomach. My skin feels acutely aware of him and my eyes glance down at his lips. Having forgotten to breathe, I inhale sharply.

Tony gently grazes his lips on my cheek and then he steps away. I don't want him to and neither does he, but he doesn't want to take advantage of me in such a turbulent time. "Your eyes are black now," he whispers matter-of-factly.

I blush at being caught reading his emotions.

Not bothered by it at all, he asks boldly, "Will you allow me to come with you to find Dr. Hastings and Zack?"

I nod my head at the same time that I say, "Yes."

"Then it's a date," he says, before realizing how funny that sounded in such a circumstance. "I mean, it's a deal."

I actually let off a half smile. "I get it."

The corner of his mouth tips upward as well. "I

better go get us some supplies then. If you plan to go today then you'd better get some food in your stomach. I won't have you passing out on me."

"Deal." I feel the first starts of something semi-decent inside, knowing that we are going to be taking action.

"Why don't you wash up first and change? I'll meet you in the cafeteria." He heads towards the door.

"Okay." I wait till he leaves, then I head to the bathroom to take a quick shower.

FIVE

I manage to keep down a peanut butter sandwich.

Tony meets me in the empty cafeteria. He carries two backpacks and holds a pistol in his hand. He walks up to my table and seems pleased with the fact that I've finally eaten something. He places the pistol on the table.

I get up from the table and start to grab the pistol, but then I hear someone clear their throat. I turn to find my dad.

"Tony told me you were leaving." He looks exhausted with bags under his bloodshot eyes and more grey than usual in his hair.

Nerves rise up as I nod. "I have to, Dad."

"I'll come with you," he offers.

Tony and I both say in unison, "No."

My dad looks like he wants to argue so I say, "You have to stay with Sebastian. You can't leave him."

"You don't have to go," he urges me.

"Yes, Dad, I do."

He holds my gaze for several seconds and then pulls something from his pocket. He holds out a white, sealed envelope to me. "Your mother left this for you."

I look down at it like it's a hallucination or something that I can't quite comprehend. My dad pushes it closer to me and I have no choice but to take it from his grasp.

"You can read it when you're ready." I stare down at the envelope, not knowing what to say. It feels much heavier than it is, as if it weighs a thousand pounds.

My dad pulls me into a hug, crushing the envelope and me into him. "You have to come home to me." The emotion is so thick it chokes his words.

"I will, Dad." I hold on tight with my free hand.

He doesn't let go for several seconds and when we part, he looks to Tony. "You will take care of my girl, right?"

"Yes sir," Tony says solidly.

"You will bring her back to me safe and sound?" My dad seems so tired as he questions him.

"I will protect her with my life," Tony vows.

My dad's eyes water and all he can do is nod. He looks at me one last time and says, "I love you, Willow."

"I love you too, Dad." With that, I watch him walk away.

I look back down at the wrinkled envelope in my hand. I turn it over a few times in silent thought before stuffing it into the back pocket of my jeans. My dad said to read it when I'm ready. Right now, I'm not ready. I have something to do first. "Let's do this," I tell Tony as I pick up the pistol from the table and grab a backpack from him.

Tony nods his head firmly and then leads the way out of the cafeteria and out of the hotel.

The day is coming to an end and twilight is in full swing. I'm glad for the timing; it means when we get to the prison grounds it will be nightfall.

The air has a cool snap to it. One that tells me that winter may still come despite the plans to unleash Project ELE. The wind whips my hair around my face and into my mouth. I pull it out, take a rubber band from around my wrist, and put my hair into a messy bun. I glance over at Tony, realizing he's been watching me.

"Your hair looks cute like that," he says simply.

I try not to blush but lose the battle. Instead, I playfully punch him on the arm. "Let's get out of here. We've got an appointment to make."

Tony takes my hand in his. The warmth spreads up my arm as we run, each of us pushing the other to keep at a consistent pace. We only stop a couple times to rest and get a few sips of water.

We make it to the outskirts of the prison grounds as the moon begins to rise. Again, the lights are all on at the prison, casting an unfamiliar and artificial glow. Tony and I slow our running and come to a steady walk. We move stealthily towards a group of trees that give us an unobstructed view of not only the wall, but the prison grounds behind the chain length fence as well.

"If we are going to do this, Willow," Tony whispers, turning to me. "I have to trust that you will follow these rules. I promised your dad that I would bring you home and I have full intentions of doing so." He pauses for me to respond.

"I understand," I whisper.

"Good. We need to talk to each other through our minds, no talking aloud. Number two, stay together, that's a given. Number three, we are just going to be looking around. If for some reason opportunity strikes, we have to both be in agreement on how to proceed or we leave… no arguing. I will not give that rule any leeway."

He gives a slight pause and I nod in agreement. While I may be in a hurry to wring Dr. Hastings's, and Zack's, neck, I have to be smart about it; I can't rush this.

"And the last rule, which is one of the most important. Rule number four, we squeeze each other's hand immediately if you find someone with light blue eyes. They are our only real enemy here since they can see through all abilities."

I nod my head and take a deep breath. "Got it."

"Good. Ready?" Tony asks through his thoughts.

"Yes." I swallow my nerves. I try hard not to think about what I'm going in there for. If I do, I may not follow through with my plan.

We watch a guard walk past the chain link fence. They've been walking back and forth every five minutes, almost on the dot. We wait thirty seconds and then make our move. I grab Tony's hand and turn us invisible. We run full speed towards the gate. I quickly move us through the cold metal.

This time we know where we will land when we get into the prison. We move to the brick wall and I pull Tony through it as quickly as possible. I gasp on the other side when I find the room that we enter into completely empty.

"Where are they?" I ask Tony.

"Who?" He looks around the empty, concrete-walled room.

I forgot that Tony wasn't with us when we first entered the prison. "This is where they were keeping a lot of the others; the one's that didn't have that reaction on the tests."

Tony visibly shivers. "They must have moved them."

"I hope that's the case and not something worse." Our people need to find a way to rescue those prisoners soon. If there are any prisoners left to rescue that is. Ice shivers run down my spine and I fight back the thought.

"Let's keep moving." Tony pulls me towards the door.

I walk us through to the other side, finding the hallway empty. We walk quickly down the cellblock. The jail cell, where I placed the guard I knocked out, is empty. I wonder how long it took them to find him.

We walk to the next set of doors and I pull Tony through. Thankfully, no guards are walking down this hall either. It seems eerily deserted.

We check each window, looking for Dr. Hastings or Zack, who are nowhere to be found as of yet. This time when we walk through the steel doors, we run straight through the hall of curtains to the other side. The bulb that flickered creepily last time has finally given up and the entire room is dark except for the minimal light coming in through the windows near the ceiling. My stomach rolls sickly as I remember the small, curtained room with blood splatters all over it.

We go through the next two sets of doors as quietly as possible, knowing what's on the other side. As we step through the final door, we are plunged into darkness. A lone light shines at the far end of the room in an office. The cubicles and break room are empty and deathly quiet.

"Where are all of the people?" I wonder in my head.

Thinking I was asking him the question, Tony answers, "It's late, maybe they are off for the night." He gestures his head towards the end of the giant room where the single light is on. "Someone might be pulling an all-nighter though. We need to be careful."

I nod my head and we start walking towards the light. When we round the last cubicle, we see the small corner office where the light shines. We crouch down low trying to get a peek inside the doorway. It doesn't look like anyone is home. We stand back up and hear a muffled cough and then furious typing on a keyboard.

I inch closer to the doorway and peek around the corner before Tony can pull me back. My heart jumps.

"Breaking the rules!" Tony demands.

I focus on breathing. "Dr. Hastings is in there... Alone."

Tony's expression turns from serious to angry. "We may not get an opportunity like this again." I watch him use his free hand to pull the gun out.

I pull mine out as well. My hand is shaking. "I agree." Will I be able to kill him though? That's the main question.

"You don't have to do this. You can stand here. I can take him out and you don't have to raise a hand." He urges me with his eyes to let him do this.

"No! I need to do this myself." I take a deep breath.

"Let's stay invisible though. He doesn't need to see us coming. We don't want him to sound any alarms." Tony holds his gun out and grabs the crook of my elbow, knowing I need both hands to aim my gun.

I straighten up and step out slowly into the doorway. I raise my gun and line my sights on the back of Dr. Hastings's head. He doesn't know I'm here. I could do away with him with a slight pull of my index finger. My hand starts shaking and my chest tightens. Something dark starts filling me. A part of me wants to let the darkness fill me to the brim. Another part wants to fight it off. I slowly lower my pistol but Hastings scratches the back of his head and I raise it back up. "I don't know if I can do it." I keep my pistol trained on his grey hair.

"Let me." Tony raises his gun.

"Only a coward would shoot a person in their back." Dr. Hastings slowly turns around. His blue eyes land on me. The same eyes his daughter has.

My eyes widen in surprise and I'm not sure what to do. I keep my gun pointed at his head. He didn't have blue eyes yesterday.

"Yes, I figured I needed this gift if I were going to have any advantage around you." Dr. Hastings answers my unspoken question.

Tony lets go of my arm and I let go of the invisibility since it does us no good here.

"So, are you going to say hi or anything? Or are you just going to kill me in cold blood?" Hastings asks.

"Hands above your head," Tony demands.

Dr. Hastings slowly raises his hands up and places them on the back of his head. He leans back looking way too comfortable in a situation like this.

I finally find my voice and answer his earlier question. "I'm not killing you in cold blood. An eye for an eye, Doctor."

The fact that he has the nerve to actually laugh makes the prospect of shooting him seem all the more appealing. "Your mother killed herself, Willow. That wouldn't be an eye for an eye."

Anger flashes inside me like lightning. "No! You killed her! You and your son killed her. You held that shot to her neck."

"Yes, but we didn't have any intention of killing either of your parents. We only wanted a simple pint of blood from you. It was an empty threat." He tries to soften his expression but I don't buy it.

"If it was an empty threat then there wouldn't have been anything deadly in that shot." I'm not stupid enough for him to manipulate me with doubts.

He shrugs his shoulders. "I'm truly sorry that your mom died. I had no idea she would have reacted in such a way."

I narrow my eyes. "You aren't sorry. You are a

horrible excuse for a human being."

He clucks his tongue. "You don't even know me, Willow. I can help you."

"Oh yeah! Like you helped seal my friends in a cave? Like you helped try to make me into your own personal lab experiment? Like you killed my mom? Or like you created all of these abilities and basically tested it out on all of us? You don't care who gets hurt. You even killed your own wife!" My voice gradually grows louder as I throw each accusation at him.

"Don't speak of things you don't know about, little girl!" Dr. Hastings throws his hands down on the table loudly. His face turns beet red. I guess I must have pushed the right button.

Tony steps forward with his gun trained on him. "Hands up now!" he demands.

Dr. Hastings gives him a mean look but complies with his demand. It takes him a few seconds but his face goes slack again like he couldn't be concerned with all of this. "You may not think I can help you but I can. You just have to give me a simple pint of blood."

I don't respond to him because I know he can't do a thing for me.

"I know how to help a person you care deeply for," he adds.

My eyes widen in shock and my heart starts racing.

"Yes, you know what I mean, don't you?" Dr. Hastings says in his attempt at playful banter.

"What is he talking about, Willow?" Tony asks me.

I shake my head at him. "Nothing. The man is crazy."

Hastings laughs. I roll my eyes and give him a furious glare. He smiles as he says, "I can undo it, simple as that. For a measly pint of your blood."

"Enough! You aren't getting anything from her." Tony turns to me. "Let me do this, Willow." His fingers inch toward the trigger.

I look from him to Dr. Hastings and then back to Tony. I have no reason to trust that Dr. Hastings can help Tony. I should just kill him, but I realize that I'm not going to be able to. Not with this new possibility that he laid out on the table. "I can't."

"Then I will." Tony walks around the desk and points the barrel of the gun at Dr. Hastings's temple. "Say goodnight."

His eyes narrow and for once he actually looks appropriately scared. He looks at me with a disgusted glare. "You Mosby women are nothing but trouble. I should have killed you when I had the chance. I don't even know what my boy saw in you. If he were here, I'd make him kill you," he spits.

I don't even pay attention to the part about Zack. I can only focus on his negative indication of my mother. I yell, "My mom did nothing to you!"

"With only a few words that woman started an uprising in here! Promising all of those workers that she would free them."

Pride wells within me for my mom. I smile and it

pisses Dr. Hastings off even more.

"Can I proceed?" Tony asks one last time.

I appreciate that he wants to make sure he doesn't take this right away from me in case I feel like I need to be the one to kill him. "No. Knock him out. We will take him with us and show him what it's like to be a prisoner."

Tony starts to nod his head but then his body goes rigid and his eyes focus on something behind me. That's when I feel the cold metal of a barrel land on the back of my head.

I don't see the man behind me nor do I recognize his voice when he begins making demands. "Put your gun down now or she dies!"

Tony's expression hardens as he stares the man down. He slowly moves to place the gun on the table but before he does, he asks. "Do you trust me, Willow?"

I don't even have to think about it. "I do."

"Then duck!" he yells into my head.

Without hesitation, I drop to the ground. In the same instant, Tony raises his gun back up in a flash and shoots the man in the chest. The guard drops to the ground dead.

In my peripheral vision, I watch Dr. Hastings pull a gun out from under his desk. In the second that he aims it at Tony, I raise my gun without hesitation, aim it and shoot. I watch in horror as the doctor's eyes turn vacant. The small red dot on the corner of his forehead looks so harmless. Like a small cut that could be covered with a Band-Aid. I don't realize that I'm not breathing until the dizziness washes over me. I blink two times and then take a deep breath.

Tony moves quickly to my side and takes the gun from my shaking hands. He puts it away and pulls me into him. My whole body is shaking and inside I don't know how I feel. "Dr. Hastings is dead. I killed him." I keep repeating in my head. "I killed him. I killed him."

"I know, Willow. You did the right thing. You saved my life." He holds me tightly and gingerly brushes my hair through his fingers. "We need to get moving. Those shots will certainly draw some attention if anyone is around to hear them. We're still not sure if Zack's even here, so we should get out while we can."

I nod my head because my voice is lost. He takes my shaky hand in his and I use the last of my resources to turn us invisible. We move through the walls and away from the prison, the place of my nightmares. By the time we reach the tree line, my body is trembling so heavily that Tony pulls his hand from mine and lifts me into his arms. He begins running in the direction of the safe house. With the last of my energy, I rise from his arms and ask him, "Please don't take me to the safe house. I want to go somewhere alone, somewhere with you." Tony eyes me suspiciously for a moment but nods his head in agreement. I rest my head back on his chest and let myself go.

SIX

I wake up wrapped up in a cozy quilt with the fire lit in the fireplace.

I have no clue where I'm at but it looks to be some sort of rustic log cabin. I catch a glimpse of Tony out of the corner of my eye. He's standing over a small gas camping stove, warming a mug that's begun to steam.

He must sense me waking up because he turns in my direction. His eyes light up upon seeing me. He makes his way over and hands me the cup, handle first.

I wrap my hands around it, finding comfort in the warmth it provides. "Thanks," I say.

Tony perches on the edge of the couch. I lift my head up and take a drink. "Ramen noodles," I say excitedly. "Where did you get this? I haven't been able to get my hands on any of this for years!" I sip the broth, reveling in its flavor. I close my eyes, "Mmm, chicken flavored."

Tony shakes his head and chuckles. "This is where I used to live." He pauses for a moment to let it sink in. "My parents and I liked the quiet and moved to this cabin a few years before ELE. When you asked me to go somewhere else last night, this was the first place to pop into my mind.

Anyway, we always tried to keep a few items around that were imperishable. Ramen was a definite option for that reason." All the while, I'm gulping the broth and loudly slurping the noodles. "And I guess I'm glad I did because apparently, I just made your year!"

I nod my head, taking sip after sip of this glorious liquid. I get to the bottom of my cup way too soon and hold it out for him... hoping he has more.

"Slow down there, slugger, you're gonna get sick," he playfully scolds me.

"Great, now you know my weakness..." I jest playfully. He takes my cup and refills it once more. Again, I gobble it down in less than a minute.

Tony goes over and jabs at the fire, making it spark and crackle. It feels like I'm a world away in this cabin. Everything seems so... normal. All the loss and heartache I've experienced in the past few days has been left outside. But then a cloud comes over my eyes, bringing with it the thunderstorms. I still have to figure out how to help Tony. I haven't the slightest clue as to how a person transitions into a Reaper... I've only heard that it happens within a few days. I just hope my healing ability stalls the inevitable. I make it my mission to make these last days with Tony some of his best. I can't sit here and feel sorry for him or I'll miss the opportunity at hand to make him happy. I want that to be the last free memories he has. My mom would have wanted that for him as well. I shift the heartache and memories of the last two days to the far recesses of my mind.

Tony places the poker next to the fire and grabs a book. "Do you want me to read to you?" he asks me.

I can't even think how long ago it was that someone read to me. "Sure," I say shrugging my shoulders. "Why not." I set the coffee cup on the table beside me and curl back up into the quilt. Tony moves a large wooden rocking chair over to where I'm at and takes a seat. "So, what are you reading to me?" I ask.

He chuckles. "Alice in Wonderland. It's one of my favorites."

"Mine too," I whisper.

Tony gets comfortable in his chair and opens the old, tattered book. He clears his throat and begins, "Alice was beginning to get very tired of sitting by her sister on the bank, and of having nothing to do: once or twice she had peeped into the book her sister was reading, but it had no pictures or conversations in it, 'and what is the use of a book,' thought Alice 'without pictures or conversation?'"

I snicker when he says Alice's lines in a girly voice.

"What?" he asks me now that I've clearly interrupted him with my giggling. He narrows his eyes at me playfully and looks like he's going to pounce when all of a sudden his face goes lax. He stares into the distance, his eyes filled with hollowed emotion.

"Tony," I say trying to figure out how he can go from all emotion to nothing, so quickly. I wave my hand in front of his eyes, but still no response.

Suddenly he gets up from the rocking chair and walks into the kitchen, his usual gait absent. He opens one of the drawers in the kitchen area and pulls out a large butcher knife, leaving the drawer open. He turns robotically towards me, butcher knife in hand.

"Uh, Tony... what are you doing?" I ask him one last time before I start to panic. Naturally he doesn't answer and it dawns on me that Tony isn't in control here... something else is. I scoot back on the couch and crouch with my legs underneath me. Not knowing what I'm battling against I want to be ready for anything. And I have to do it just right or I could injure the Tony that's buried deep inside.

As Tony comes closer, I look him in the eyes. I notice a small red swirl, almost like a tornado, circling his iris.

"The shot," I say breathlessly. Like a lion about to pounce its prey, I ready myself to move. When Tony is but five feet from me, he begins raising the knife. I move quickly until I'm behind him and immediately grab his hand. His grip is deathly tight. I squeeze his wrist like he taught me and disarm the knife from his grasp. It falls to the ground and I kick it across the room. Then I immediately focus on healing, hoping with all I am that I can heal him again.

It only takes a few seconds before Tony, the real Tony, comes back to me. I slide off his back landing softly on the wooden floor. He turns to look at me, his face contorted in utter confusion. "What..." he asks, searching for words. "What was that?"

I scratch my head noticing the absence of the red in his eyes. "Uh, you were giving me a piggy back ride." I want to hit myself in the forehead for giving such a stupid answer but it was the only thing that came to my mind.

He ponders this for a moment and, surprisingly, he just shrugs his shoulders.

He looks lost in thought so I suggest, "Hey, let's read more of Alice in Wonderland."

He still looks perplexed, but he nods and sits back down in the rocking chair picking up the book from the floor.

While he's busy looking for where to start I walk inconspicuously over to where the knife is on the floor and silently kick it under the couch. I quickly slide onto the couch and throw the quilt up over my lap. I'm out of breath and sweating a little from the 'incident'.

Tony reads a few chapters and the entire time I find it hard to focus on the story at hand. I can't help staring at Tony and expecting him to just snap again. What the flip was that? I wonder. Out of all of the reactions I could have expected someone turning into a Reaper to do, I wouldn't have thought of that. I mean, if he's blacking out and going into Reaper mode or whatever, why did he grab a knife? Wouldn't he just try to take my powers with his touch? It doesn't take a knife to do that.

I glance towards the kitchen and can't help but wonder if I should hide the butcher block of knifes sitting on the counter. But, if we're being honest, he could use anything as a weapon.

"Are you okay, Willow?" Tony asks me.

I shake my head to clear it and look back at Tony. "Yeah... I mean, yes. I think so." I pride myself on the fact that I didn't bust out and yell, "No, you're turning into a Reaper," like I wanted to.

He stands up and puts the book away, then comes and sits next to me on the couch. "You just seem a little lost in thought." He pulls part of the blanket over his legs too. "You know, it's alright for you to admit that you aren't okay. You've been through so much in the past few days, what with losing your mom and then killing Dr. Hastings. That's a whole heck of a lot to sift through."

I grunt nervously. "Well then, I guess I should be real and admit that I'm all screwed up inside." My fake smile drops. "You're right, I'm not okay, but I'm working on finding a way to cope. I have to get through this and I'm very thankful to have you here with me right now." I run my hand through my hair.

"I know you'll be able to find a way to cope, Willow. You are stronger than you know. I remember when I lost my parents. At first, I was so mad at them for turning into Reapers and trying to turn me into one too. I hated them. I hated them because of their actions; your mom was forced to kill them. I was pretty screwed up inside back then too. Day by day though, things started easing up. I felt a little more like myself as time passed. Things will never be the same, but at least I know that I survived it. I know you will survive this just fine and come out even stronger because of it." Tony pulls me towards him on the couch and places his arm around me.

I rest my head on his shoulder and sigh. "I hope so. It's interesting the turmoil going on inside me. Part of my brain wants to close my eyes and pretend like nothing ever happened. Another part of me wants to break down and cry forever or to get angry at the world and take my pain out on everything in my path. Yet, I find myself in a strange limbo between all of these emotions. I find myself wanting to just move on. I don't want to sit and comprehend everything that has happened. I don't want to miss my mom or feel guilty for taking a life, even though he would have taken yours if I hadn't shot him. I just want to be. Because if I can just find a way to just be, I can get through this..." I let out a loud breath. "Wow, none of that just made sense. I should just shut up."

Tony squeezes me gently. "No, actually it makes a lot of sense." We sit in silence for a few minutes. It's not awkward. Instead, it's kind of peaceful. Tony asks a few minutes later, "Do you want to go back to the safe house?"

I sit up and look at him. "Is it okay if we stay here a little while longer? I think I just need some time away from everyone's attention. I don't think I could take it having my friends hover over me asking if I'm okay all of the time. You know?"

Tony laughs softly. "Kind of like how I asked you if you are okay just now?"

I give him a half grin. "No, that's not what I mean."

Tony smiles back. "Yeah, I guess I'm the exception."

"Yes, you are the exception." I nod my head.

He gives me a smoldering look that makes me feel warm and fuzzy inside. "You know I'd do anything for you, right?" Tony asks me.

I give him a small, but meaningful, smile. "I know you would. You've always been there when I needed you. But I do have to warn you. Now that you've said it out loud I may have to cash in on it sometime."

He gives me a light laugh. "If you say so," he says playfully.

"So," I say changing the subject. "If we are going to stick around here for a little while longer, I guess I ought to give you the grand tour." He stands up and holds his hand out for me.

"Why, I'd be honored." I accept his hand and he pulls me up from the couch. The blanket falls to the ground. I pick it up and place it back on the sofa. That's when I see some dried blood on my inner wrist.

Tony notices it too and gently pulls my arm up to get a better look. "What happened? When did you cut yourself?"

I look down, not sure what to say. You can barely see a scar from where the knife must have sliced me without my knowledge. My healing abilities must have fixed me up. "I don't know, it probably happened last night."

Tony looks at me suspiciously. I don't waver so finally he says, "Let's get you cleaned up then first." He takes me to the kitchen and washes my arm under the sink. I watch as he gently wipes at the bloodstain with a damp cloth. I could have just as easily rinsed my own arm off but something about Tony's gesture and protective qualities is quite endearing in this moment.

After I'm all cleaned up and good to go, no Band-

Aid necessary, he takes me on the tour. I view their formal dining room, which consists of a large oak table and six chairs. He takes me upstairs and shows me his parent's room, which he doesn't linger in too long. I'm sure the memories in there are hard for him.

I give him a hug after we close the door. "So can I see your room?"

The grief leaves his eyes and turns quickly into playfulness. "I thought you'd never ask." He takes me down the hall and opens the door to his room. I walk in and look around. It's definitely not what I would have expected. The pitched ceiling makes the room look open and airy. A full size bed sits in the corner. A large desk seems to be the main focal point of the room. On it sits numerous graphite pencils, papers of different texture and colors, paints and a few books on sketching. Sketches of people and cars hang on the walls.

"Did you draw all of these?" I walk into the room and look from picture to picture as if browsing in an art exhibit.

"Yes," Tony whispers. I look back at him and I can see something in his expression. His cheeks are a little red and he looks almost embarrassed.

"They are beautiful. You have amazing talent," I reassure him.

His expression lightens and he smiles meekly, which is surprising since nothing about Tony is meek. "Thanks. I wasn't sure if you'd think it was goofy or childish."

I shake my head and go back to admiring his

handiwork. "Nothing about art is childish. Not many people can draw like this." A sketch of an old Lamborghini is so three dimensional and starkly real that it looks like it could drive right off the paper. I find a picture of a man and woman holding hands. They look so lively and in love. The shading is perfect and you can see the emotions in their faces. The love shines through in the drawing. "Who is this?" I ask.

Tony comes to stand next to me. "That's my parents." He reaches out and gently grazes the sketch with his fingertips.

"They must have been very much in love." I'm not sure if this subject is too painful or if I should move us on to another sketch or not.

"They were. You know, I've had some time to think about it. I think that might have been part of the reason they turned into Reapers. I think they thought it would give them the best advantage to stay alive and together longer. We didn't know how long or how hot the temperatures would get during that time. When the first set of people started turning with that red shot, they tried to convince others that it was the best thing for everyone. They spoke about feeling more powerful than ever and some even thought that the change would make them immortal. When my parents made the decision, it was before everyone realized how bad Reapers really were. Some people were already dying around the shelter and coming up brain dead, but they didn't know it was because of a Reaper. I think the sudden deaths were a catalyst to my parents' choice as well as many others. I honestly believe that my mom and dad were trying to find a way to make sure they both survived together, along with me. I don't think they were looking for power. It's kind of ironic that little did they know that the change would kill the very love they were working so hard to protect." He turns away from the sketch.

What a tragic love story, I think to myself. I look up and notice his eyes are watering. I pull him into a hug. We stand there in each other's embrace for several seconds, neither of us wanting to let go. Tony leans back to where we are still in each other's arms but he can now look into my eyes.

I get caught up in that look and it nearly takes my breath away. So much can be said without words. I glance down at his lips and without my even thinking of it, I start leaning forward.

Tony clears his throat and takes a step back. "Why don't we go get some air?"

An ounce of hurt flashes inside me but I remind myself that Tony and I are just friends. I know he liked me like that once, but I made it known I wasn't into him in that way. He has no reason to be still into me. Plus, enough is going on right now. I don't need to be thinking about Tony in that way; especially when I just broke up with my first love not even two days ago. "Air sounds good," I say.

I follow Tony out of his room, down the stairs and out the front door. I find myself in stunned awe at the view outside. When we arrived last night I was not only pretty out of it, but it was also pitch black so I couldn't see anything.

I step down from the porch and start walking towards the most magical lake I've ever seen. The sun causes the calm water to glisten. Mountains stand up in the background at the far end of the lake. Their image is cast onto the gentle water perfectly and the wisps of white clouds and blue sky above them give the reflection even more depth. I walk all the way to the water's edge, mesmerized by the setting. "I could live out here."

"I could see you living out here too. This is my favorite place on Earth." Tony puts his hand on the small of my back.

"I can see why," I tell him.

We take a seat on the soft grass and watch the clouds float over the water as if it's the best show in the world.

An hour must pass at least, with how long we sit in silence until Tony speaks. "Can I ask you a question, Willow?"

"Shoot." I turn to him.

He looks at me as if gauging how he should ask this. That can't be a good sign. "Why did Alec and you break up?"

Not a question I was expecting, but I'm sure it was a question that's been on his mind. "Um... I wasn't really the best girlfriend, you know."

Tony lets out a light huff. "I doubt that."

I raise my eyebrow. "Seriously, I wasn't. I did some stuff behind his back and I should have trusted him by letting him know what I was doing. I'm not sure why I didn't tell him that I was going to go after my parents or why I didn't just let him come, but I can't really go back in time and fix it. I made the decision and I doubt even if I could go back in time that I would have brought him into that mess."

"Why didn't you just apologize?" he asks as if it were that simple.

"There was more to it. I kept stuff like that from him before in the shelter too. Also, he felt like I was keeping something else from him. I think that was the main reason we broke up." I bite my lip knowing his next question.

"What else were you keeping from him?"

"He thinks I have feelings for someone else," I say.

Tony's eyes widen as the truth sets in. "Do you?" he asks a little breathlessly.

"I think maybe so." I look away shyly. The truth can be so awkward.

"Oh," Tony whispers.

My eyes dart back to his and I instinctively bite my lip. I wonder what 'oh' means. Good, bad? I quickly say, "Anyhow, I'm not ready to really dive into that right now. I have enough on my plate." I expect to see some relief in his eyes but instead he looks a little disappointed. That actually makes me feel better, knowing that he likes the fact that I might be feeling something for him.

Tony stands to his feet and helps me to mine. "Well, if we're going to have anything good to eat tonight we'd better get to work."

I give him a smirk. "I don't really mind having Ramen again," I playfully suggest.

Tony gives a small chuckle. "Ramen doesn't exactly give your body what it needs to function. Come on, I'll show you how to get a real dinner."

I follow Tony through the woods quietly while he sets snares and traps made from string, rocks, and twigs. I watch as he sets them up, one by one. His muscles strain against his shirt, which makes the shirt look like it's about to lose the battle and rip. Tony catches me staring at his arms and I quickly look away, clearing my throat.

I follow him as he wanders through the woods that he knows like the back of his hand. He takes me past a few Pine trees to where his favorite blackberry bush is. I taste one and it's perfectly ripe and sweet. We decide to take some back to the cabin with us. My hands get full trying to carry them all, so Tony takes his shirt off and makes a sort of satchel to carry the berries in. When he tries to hand it to me, I don't notice; I'm too busy trying to figure out if he has a six-pack or a twelve pack. Catching me in a semi-stalkerish moment, he clears his throat. I snap out of it, blushing from head to toe. Embarrassing! I take his shirt and focus on filling it to the brim with blackberries.

After we've picked the bush almost clean, leaving some for the animals, we head over to another clearing where he teaches me about wild greens and what you can and can't eat. We find Stinging Nettle, Chickweed, Dandelion and Monkey Flowers. I've never eaten any of them before so I'm looking forward to this culinary adventure.

We double back to where Tony set the traps and find a rabbit caught in one of the snares. Tony picks it up by the ears. He must see the look on my face because he says, "Think of it as food, Willow. Not a cute, furry pet."

I nod my head but my face still says eeekkk. I stand on the other side of Tony, as far away from little bunny foo foo as I can. It creeps me out knowing what's about to come next.

Tony sends me with a pail to collect water and directions to the well so I can clean the things we gathered. He tells me that the water line from the well is clogged so I will have to get water the old-fashioned way.

Tony stays behind to 'prepare' the rabbit. I guess prepare is the nice people word for butcher. My stomach churns a little with the thought. Don't think about it, Willow, I tell myself.

I locate the well easily. Pushing back the cover, I attach the bucket to the hook at the top and slowly lower it down. It's interesting because I've never had to use a well before for water. I guess this cabin is too far out to be connected to the city water. Retrieving the water turned out to be pretty easy. I squat down next to the well and begin cleaning all of the greens and blackberries we're having for dinner.

I keep hearing Tony, up near the house, chopping on a stump. Images in my head of a furry bunny staring back at me from my dinner plate play across my mind. Gross.

After I'm through cleaning, I gather up everything, along with a clean bucket of water for Tony to clean up his…er…mess. He sees the bucket and smiles, "I wondered when you were coming back. I started worrying you may have fallen into the well."

I roll my eyes and hand him the bucket. "I didn't want to see bunny foo foo chopped to bits, okay?"

He gives me a sideways grin. "Bunny foo foo?" he asks. It sounds funny coming from him. "You named our dinner?"

I finally give in and laugh. It does sound pretty ridiculous.

I head into the house as Tony washes up the blood bath. I find two large bowls, one to put the salad greens in and one to but the blackberries in. I steal a couple berries and put them in my mouth. The sweet, savory juice slides down my throat. Mmm, so good!

Tony comes through the door with a skewered, butchered rabbit on a long stick. He places the stick in the fireplace on these two 'legs' that connect with a crank. He adds a few more logs to the fire and gets a good, strong flame going. "We'll want to crank that every few minutes or so to keep it from burning."

I nod while admiring how self-sufficient Tony is… and his biceps. Shaking my head, I clear the cobwebs and finish the task at hand. I grab a blackberry from the bowl and squat down next to Tony. "Open your mouth and close your eyes," I say to him. I swallow the knot that's formed in my throat. My mother used to say that to me when I was little.

Tony turns towards me and gives me an impish grin. He abides and opens his mouth, keeping his eyes tightly shut. I place the blackberry in his mouth but all I see are his lips. They're hypnotizing. I move my fingers from his mouth and watch as he bites into the blackberry. His mouth turns up at the corners, "It's sweet."

I break out of my trance when he opens his eyes and I nod my head in agreement. He turns the crank a few more times till the browned side is pointing upwards. Tony is illuminated by the firelight casting beautiful shadows across his face. The glow makes each of his features more prominent and that much more attractive to look at. He turns towards me and I watch his yellow eyes gain depth and meaning. He reaches out and touches the side of my cheek. My eyes instantly close and I revel in his touch. He places a piece of my hair back behind my ears and lets his fingers trace the line of my cheekbone all the way down to my chin.

I open my eyes at the absence of his touch.

"You're so beautiful, Willow."

I bite my lower lip.

He says this in all seriousness and I believe him. Breaking the moment, he stands and holds his hand out to me. I take it and he helps me up. "The salad dressing isn't going to make itself," he says aloud.

"I wish it would," I say to myself.

"What?" Tony says, immediately turning around to face me.

My eyes go round with shock… he just heard that. "Nothing," I squeak.

He holds my gaze for a few moments longer. His

eyes filled with a silent humor. Then he turns back around to assemble the salad.

I take a long deep breath and run my hands over my face. I've got to remember we can do that.

Tony grabs some oil and vinegar and begins concocting a salad dressing. He puts a pinch of salt and pepper in it and mashes up some blackberry to make a vinaigrette. I guess I'll add: cook, to the thousand-item list of things Tony can do. I can't help but wonder if there is anything he can't do.

He reaches back under the cabinet and pulls out a jar of sugar. He breaks the seal and sprinkles some on the blackberries. I sit down on the sofa to watch the master at work. If anything, I'm in the way of this one-man show. Tony alternates between cranking the handle on the fireplace, making the salad, and setting the table. I ask him if I can help but he insists that I take it easy. He wants to make dinner for me.

I must have dozed off for a bit because Tony wakes me by gently shaking my arm. The fire has died down some and it makes me wonder how long I was out. As if knowing what I'm thinking he answers me, "You were only out about half an hour."

I nod my head and sit up. Wiping my eyes, I let out a yawn. "It smells good…"

"Well it should, I made it," Tony says with confidence.

I follow him into the dining area where he's set up two plates… and a candle in the middle. The butterflies flutter in my stomach when it reminds me of that candlelight dinner we shared a while back. Only this time is different. This time not only am I single, but we're also alone. That ups the ante a bit.

I go to take a seat and Tony comes up from behind me, pulling out my chair. I sit down and he gracefully helps me scoot forward. He takes a seat and serves both of us our portions. I grab my fork and knife and try out the rabbit first. It's good; not at all gamey like I thought it would be. The salad is divine and it goes perfectly with it. A girl could sure get used to this kind of cooking! Tony mentions in between bites to save room for dessert.

After dinner, Tony brings out a dessert of warm blackberries with a sugary crumble mixture on top. It's absolutely ridiculous. I savor every bite.

We've been mostly silent throughout the meal and I decide to break the rhythm with some conversation. "So, are you going to tell me how you learned to cook?"

Tony finishes chewing his bite of food before answering. "Surprisingly, I learned from my dad. He went to culinary school in New York. Back when the virus wasn't a threat. He started teaching me the moment I could reach the counter. My mom also loved to bake. That double oven was a gift to her for their fifth wedding anniversary. She said it was one of the best gifts she ever received, with the exception of me." Tony stares off at the stove, lost in a memory.

I place my hand over his on the table. "It sounds like your parents were pretty amazing."

Tony looks back at me. The pain is still evident. "They were actually. It's hard for me sometimes to connect the past them with the people they turned into after taking that shot." He looks down at the table and drums his fork against it nervously with his free hand. "I shouldn't admit it but honestly Willow; deep down in my heart I am happy that Dr. Hastings is dead." He looks back up at me and finishes. "Anyone who had it in their right mind to create a substance that can cause that sort of reaction such as it did with the Reapers, deserves that fate."

I take a deep breath. "I wish I could say that I don't agree with you. That taking a life is taking a life no matter what sins they've committed. But, I can't help feeling like the world is just that much safer with him gone."

"I agree," Tony says stoically. "So... this is pretty heavy conversation for our first date."

I look at him in surprise. "Oh really? I didn't know this was a date."

He gives me a crooked smile that makes him look that much more handsome. "I figure it is if you'd like it to be."

I think about it for a few moments. I don't know if I'm ready for dating yet. "Maybe we can call it that. I mean you did cook for me and all. As long as we take things slow, like a sloth crossing the street kind of slow."

He laughs at my analogy. "Yeah, that can be a-rr-a-n-g-e-d," he says in a slow motion voice.

I slap him on the hand and we both chuckle. We talk more about our childhood while we finish the incredible desert. I go back for seconds, not caring if I look like a glutton.

After dinner, Tony tells me to sit on the couch. I watch him run up the stairs. He returns a minute later with a six-string guitar in his hand.

"Oh, you're that guy?" I joke aloud.

Tony arches his eyebrow. "What kind of guy are you referring to?"

"You know, the guy who can do everything. Cook, draw, play instruments, kick butt and everything else under the sun. Not only are you unbelievably good looking but you have to have all of this talent too? I feel a little inadequate."

Tony smiles and seems to chew on it for a few seconds before he says, "Sometimes I snore, I absolutely loath doing the dishes, I can't sing a note, I have a double cowlick so if I don't keep my hair cut short my hair will stand pitch straight on the back of my head and I don't really like cats. I mean, I love kittens, but cats kind of creep me out."

I can't help but grin from ear to ear. "Oh, so there is a chink in all of that armor?" I laugh. "By the way, cats kind of creep me out too. I mean, one second they are loving on you and the next they try to scratch out your eyeballs."

Tony laughs. "Yep!" He grins and sits down on the hearth of the fireplace with his guitar on his lap. "So back to your original statement... you think I'm good looking?"

Duh! He looks extremely hot with his guitar and

his messy copper hair. "I think you know very well that the looks decent wagon didn't pass you by."

He smiles. "Well, since we are being honest, I have to admit that I think you are so beautiful and sometimes when I look at you, you take my breath away." He gives me a sobered expression that melts my insides.

I open my mouth but no words come out. I hold his gaze and then, feeling a little intimidated, I look down at my fingernails. Tony starts strumming the guitar and I sway to the sound of the strings.

We talk a little more throughout the night and when I start to get sleepy, Tony begins playing his guitar again while I curl up on the couch. I fall asleep to the gentle, strumming lullaby.

I can't breathe!

The fact that I'm suffocating, pulls me from the dreamy state I was in. My eyes shoot open and my hands flail out. When I recognize Tony on top of me with his hands clenched hard around my neck, my heart starts hammering. The red in his eyes is swirling like torpedoes, going this way and that. His expression is that of someone not fully connected with reality, as he does his best to block off my airway.

I throw my hands over his and try to pull them away from my neck but no luck; he's much stronger than I am. Stars dance across my eyes as the edge of my vision begins to blur. My lungs beg for air and I try fighting harder. I dig my nails into the skin of his hands. He doesn't flinch. Tears come to my eyes as I realize my time is dwindling down. I can't get him off me and I can't breathe! "Please stop Tony! Please!" I beg.

His grip loosens a little and I think maybe some part of him deep inside, may have heard my plea. I breathe what little air I can through the small airway he's allowed with his lightened grip. It's barely enough to fill half of my lungs before he tightens down once more. He cocks his head to the side and sneers at me. "What? You don't like this, sugar?"

The realization that Tony would never in his right mind call me sugar, sends me into full fledge panic mode. I try to kick and claw at him as he squeezes my throat tighter. I swear, I can feel my vocal cords crush from the force. Stars burst forth like fireworks in my vision and a black fog starts rolling in as I continue to struggle with no real momentum, until eventually the whole world turns dark and I drift away.

I dart up, sucking in air as if it's going out of style. I look around the dark room, lit only by some dying embers in the fireplace. It takes me a few minutes to realize I'm alive and in Tony's living room. When he stirs, I turn and look down at him sleeping peacefully on the couch beside me.

What was that? A dream? A premonition? I get up, careful not to wake Tony. I make my way over to my backpack in the dark, unzipping it quietly, and grab a flashlight. I take it to the downstairs powder bath and shine it just enough to see my eyes in the mirror. They are the color of a copper penny. My heart starts beating double time as I realize that what I just went through was no dream. It's about to become a reality. I push a shaky hand through my hair.

I can't let that happen. I've never tried to change a future outcome, but I have to now! I take the flashlight and place it back inside my bag. I quietly grab my pistol from the front pocket and do my best to load a round in the chamber without waking him, and then I make my way back to the couch. I sit down on the floor facing Tony, placing the gun on the floor aimed away from me.

Closing my eyes, I focus my healing abilities. I have to heal Tony. I can't let this happen to him or to me. I place my hands gently on his chest and concentrate. I can feel a small current running from me into him. I stay there for what seems to be at least a half an hour focused completely on healing Tony.

Eventually he stirs some more and opens his eyes. He seems startled to see me sitting over him. He sits up on his elbow and my hands fall down to my knees. I feel too tired to do much of anything else with them.

"Willow? Are you okay?" he asks.

I blink a few times and then nod. "Couldn't sleep." I search his eyes for any sign of the red torpedoes but all I see is the beautiful neon yellow. Maybe it worked, I think to myself as my eyelids become heavy.

"You need to get some rest, Willow. The sun isn't even out." He pats the couch next to him and I second-guess whether the healing worked. "I'm not going to bite," Tony jokes, not knowing how scary his humor is after I just had that premonition.

Not sure what else to do, I slide onto the couch in front of him. I pull the gun towards me so it's sitting just beneath the sofa, within my reach.

Tony puts his arm around me and I tense up. He quickly throws his hand in the air. "Sorry. Are you okay,

Willow?" He sounds utterly confused.

No, I'm not okay, but I don't want him to know what happened in my premonition. If I told him, he would surely run off to protect me. I know that if he were away from me, he wouldn't stand a chance. He'd turn quickly and I wouldn't have the opportunity to stop it from happening. "Sorry, I just had a nightmare." I take his hand in mine and pull it back around me.

"Do you want to talk about it?" he whispers.

"Not tonight. I just want to sleep." I say with a yawn. I lie wide-awake until I hear Tony fall asleep. With our hands interlocked, I focus some more on healing him. I keep working on it until my eyes finally droop closed and I fall asleep too.

EIGHT

I wake up to the sun streaming in through the windows.

It takes me a moment to open my eyes. I look around for Tony since he isn't behind me. I find him packing some items into a bag.

He stops packing and smiles at me. "Good morning, sunshine."

"Morning," I say a little groggily. With the memories of last night's premonition still on the forefront of my mind, I take a few moments to try to examine him closely. From this distance, I can't see any red. Hopefully, the healing worked. If only I can heal him permanently. There has to be a way. If I can stave off this onset of the change with my healing, there has to be a way I can ramp it up to stop it for good.

I stand up and stretch my arms overhead with a yawn. "So, what's the plan?" I ask, pointing at the bag he's packing.

He looks up from what he's doing. "I'm just gathering some more supplies to take back to the safe house. Including Ramen." He holds up a couple packets to show me before he stuffs them back into the bag.

"Are we heading back today?" I ask, not sure if I really like that idea even though I know it's necessary.

"I think we ought to go let your dad know that you're safe. I'm sure he must be a nervous wreck."

My heart lurches at the thought. I hadn't really considered the worry that my absence may have caused my dad. "You're right. How far is the safe house from here?" Since I was pretty far out of it when we left the prison, I didn't get a chance to memorize the path here.

"About a half day's trip. We could get there quicker if we use our abilities." He hands me a pair of jeans, a white cotton top, and a belt. "These were my mom's. I figure you can use a change of clothes. They may be a little loose but the belt should keep everything in place.

I take the clothes and hug them to my chest. "Thanks." I wonder if it's hard for him to hand me his mom's clothes. I can't imagine handing anything that belonged to my mom to anyone else right now. Not when the loss is still so fresh.

I go to the powder room to change. When I pick up the jeans that I'd been wearing to fold them, I notice the letter in the back pocket. I had nearly forgotten it was there. I slip the envelope out and stare at it in my hands. I don't know what is inside but I still can't bring myself to open it. Opening it seems like such a final thing to do. My heart just isn't ready for it yet. I slip it into the back pocket of the new jeans. "Sorry, Mom," I whisper before heading back to find Tony.

He zips up his bag and looks up at me with a sweet

smile. "You look nice."

I pull down on my unruly curls. "Thanks."

"You ready?" He hands me a bag.

"Yes," I say. I remember the gun I had placed under the couch. I wait until Tony is preoccupied before I retrieve it. I un-chamber the bullet, put the safety on, and place it in my bag before he can notice anything out of place. I'm getting pretty good at this weapon stuff.

When we walk out of the house, I take a moment to commit the gorgeous lake view to my memory. "Do you think we will ever come back here?"

"Definitely." He takes my hand in his and we begin our long walk to the safe house.

For the most part we walk in silence, stopping only to take a sip of water. We try to keep quiet in case there are any Reapers around. We still have no idea what ever became of the Reapers out on the mountainside after Dr. Hastings turned on that noise signal.

"What about Zack?" I ask Tony.

"If you want to go after him we can." He doesn't stop and look at me, but he squeezes my hand for reassurance.

I don't know if I want to go after Zack. Killing Dr. Hastings didn't bring my mom back. I don't think taking Zack's life will do anything for me. I want to let everything stand the way it is, but I can't help but wonder if Zack may know a way to fix Tony. Perhaps I can make him tell me. Maybe now that his dad is gone and no longer controlling him, he would be willing to change like his sister. I make a note to find Candy when we get back to the safe house.

"Do you want to go after him?" he asks again since I haven't answered.

"I think I'd like to find him and talk to him. I don't want to kill him. I just want to know if he has any clue as to his father's motives for giving us all these abilities. I really want to know what he's done with all of the prisoners too. We still have a duty to help them," I answer.

We come to a place where we have to climb a small ways. Tony turns around and gives me his hand to help me up the steep hill. I accept and he helps me to the top with ease. When we are safe at the top of the hill, he says, "I think that's a wise idea. We definitely need to help the others. I can only hope that the death of Dr. Hastings could be the end of whatever evil motives he may have had."

"I hope so too." I don't have a great feeling about it though.

We run the rest of the way to the safe house in silence. We arrive right as dinner preparations are being made. We go straight to my father's room first. I knock on the door and when he opens it, he pulls me into a strong hug.

"Willow!" he says in such relief that you can hear the worry melting away. He pulls back, keeping his hands on my shoulders to examine me and make sure I'm intact.

"Yes, I told you I'd come back." I try to smile but I can't. The look of sadness and pain is still etched across his features. He looks like he hasn't eaten since I left. His eyes are bloodshot from crying.

"That you did," he says, pulling me into one last

hug. He lets me go and turns to Tony, holding out his hand. Tony shakes his hand and my dad tells him, "Thank you, son. Thank you for bringing my daughter back home safely."

"Your daughter is a very strong woman. I don't deserve much credit in bringing her home safely. She actually saved my life," Tony tells my dad.

"Is that so?" My dad turns his attention on me.

I don't answer, so Tony speaks for me. "We ran into Dr. Hastings..." My dad tenses up hearing that name. "One of his guards came in behind Willow. I took him out but Dr. Hastings made a move and Willow proved to be much faster than him. She shot him. He's dead."

My dad runs his hand through his greying hair. "He's dead?" he asks shakily.

"Yes sir," Tony tells him.

My dad stares at his feet silently for several seconds. I start to worry that maybe he's mad or disappointed that I took a life. He finally looks up at me and says, "Thank you, Willow."

My eyes water in response to those words and my shoulders drop. "I don't think I should be thanked for killing a man."

My dad puts his hands on my shoulders and forces me to look him in the eyes. "Dr. Hastings was a very bad man. He took more lives than just your mother's. Back in the shelter, we are confident that he was experimenting on some of the lower class. Many people turned up missing but none of the officials would acknowledge anything. That was the driving force of the rebellion that was beginning inside the shelter..." My father's face starts turning red. "Then, what he did to us in that clearing and in the prison... that man was a monster. He deserved to die!" He takes a deep breath then apologizes for raising his voice. "You did the right thing. You had no choice. It was either his life or Tony's."

I look from my dad to Tony and I know deep down that I wouldn't hesitate to do it again if need be. "I love you, Dad."

"I love you too." He gives me another hug.

"How is Sebastian?" I ask him.

"He's coping. He's so young so I don't think he fully understands what this means to his little world. Thankfully, children are pretty resilient. I think he'll make it through this," my dad says.

I put my hands on my dad's shoulders and make him look at me just like he did earlier, when the roles were reversed. "And you? How are you doing?"

He takes a shaky breath and his eyes water. He tries to blink back the tears but a few escape. I hate seeing such a strong man cry. I wait patiently for his response. "I'm trying, Willow. It's just so hard. Sometimes I feel like I can't take it. I feel like my heart is going to give out on me, and part of me wishes it would, so I can be with her again," he admits honestly. I don't think I've ever heard him bare his soul before.

"I feel the same way sometimes." I pull him into a hug.

He sniffs and says, "We'll get through this."

"I know, Dad, I know." I give him a gentle squeeze and let him go.

"You should go see your brother. He'll be happy that you're back," he says.

"I will. Is he still in class?" I ask, since Sebastian has been sharing a room with my dad and he's obviously not here.

"Yes, he should be downstairs with the teachers in the small conference room."

I give my dad another hug. Tony and my dad say goodbye and we leave the room in search of Sabby.

I find Sabby hunched up in a corner of the classroom. He's curled into a ball and far away from any of his other classmates. My heart goes out to him and Tony puts his arm around me. I'm not sure what to say or do so I just knock softly on the door and let myself in.

Sebastian doesn't look up from the far corner. I smile kindly at the teachers and they give me a sympathetic smile back. I walk over and crouch down low next to him. "Sabby," I whisper and touch his arm. There are tearstains running down his delicate skin.

He slowly brings his head up and as soon as he sees it's me he wraps his arms firmly around my middle, burying his head in my chest. I caress his soft curls with my hand comforting him.

"I missed you, Wello," Sabby says. He always knows what to say to bring a smile to my lips.

"I missed you too, Sabby," I say back to him. "How

about we go and get something sweet from the kitchen?"

His face perks up and he nods his head. I take his hand in mine... his soft pudgy hand. My heart breaks knowing he's going through losing our mother at such a young age. He didn't get near the amount of time I got with her. For some reason this makes me feel guilty, like I did something wrong.

I walk Sebastian over to one of the teachers and tell her I'm going to be taking him for a little bit. She pats me on the shoulder and tells us to take our time.

As I leave through the main exit, Tony is perched against a wall waiting. I crouch down to Sebastian's level. "You remember Tony, don't you?" I introduce them.

Sebastian nods his head.

"Tony's a very good friend of mine and he's going to go with us to find something sweet, okay?"

He ponders this for a moment. "Is he a very good friend like Alec is a very good friend?"

My eyes go wide with shock and my mouth falls open.

Tony snickers beside me. "You could say that," he replies for me.

I can't help but let out a small giggle.

The three of us walk to the kitchen, which is deserted except for us. I'm thankful for the emptiness. It seems like every other time I've been here it's been bustling. We begin rummaging through the cabinets and come up with a jar of honey and some spoons.

"I guess this'll have to work," I tell him. I sit Sabby

on the counter and Tony and I jump up with him. We dip our spoons into the honey and eat it lick by lick, savoring the sweetness.

"Mommy liked honey," Sabby says, breaking the silence.

"She sure did. You know what else mommy liked?" I ask him giving him a small poke in his side.

He laughs. "Wello! What else do mommy like?"

"Mommy liked things that were bright and beautiful music. She liked seeing the wind blow through the trees. She loved watching us play when we built tent houses back home. She liked to cook a big meal, even if it was only for the four of us and it was burnt to a crisp. And you know what she liked most of all?" I ask him.

He shakes his head as a drop of honey lands on his knee.

"She liked it when you smiled. It was her favorite thing in the world!" His eyes get really big.

"Weally?" he asks me.

I nod my head. "Uh-huh! She always said that you were what gave her the sparkle in her eyes."

His head drops. "I miss mommy," he says quietly.

I wrap my arm around him. "I know, Sabby, I know. I miss her too." We sit in quiet for a few moments. "But, you know what? Mommy isn't really gone. We just can't see her for a while. In fact, she's here with us right now, sitting by our side. And someday, when it's our time to go too, we'll get to see mommy again in a place where there is no more pain and no more sadness or tears." I give him a moment to let his four-year-old mind wrap around it.

His dimples show themselves as he puts a smile on his face. "I'm so happy that someday I can see mommy again," he says stumbling over his words.

"Me too, kiddo, me too."

I get Sabby cleaned up and take him back to school. He doesn't return to the corner and yet, he doesn't join the other kids right away either. One of the teachers sees him and offers to hold him. He gladly accepts and is picked up into her arms. Together they go sit down in a rocking chair and she reads him a story.

I give the room a once over before leaving. There are so many children, at least sixty in this room alone. I notice a headful of long red hair at one of the tables. Her face is set in a serious concentrating expression as she searches for the perfect piece. Lily looks like she's going to be okay. I wasn't sure how hard it would be for her to cope with her ability. It's a hard one to understand and turn off. Feeling another person's emotions is intense. I'm just glad to see her up an about since the last time I saw her she was passed out.

I look back over at Tony. He stands beside me, watching the teacher read to Sabby.

I say to him, "I hope what I said to my brother made a difference."

He touches my cheek softly. "You made all the difference in the world."

I let out a small smile, one that doesn't quite reach my eyes. "I hope so," I say as we leave.

Tony stops outside in the hall. "I need to go find

Lee. We need to attempt to rescue the prisoners again... before it's too late."

"I agree." It makes me feel good knowing that we are on the same page.

"Do you want to go with me?" he asks.

I shake my head. "No, I need to take care of a few things."

"Okay." He gives me a hug that lasts a few seconds too long... not that I'm complaining, and we part ways for the afternoon.

My first stop, find Alec.

I find him in his room reading a book. His door has been left open a few inches. I knock a few times and open it a little bit more. He gives me a comforting smile and invites me in. He places his book down, tepee style, on his bed.

I walk over to a chair in the corner of his room by his bed. "Mind if I sit?" I ask.

He shakes his head. "No, of course not."

I sit down and the comfort and familiarity of being around him warms me. I don't know exactly why I wanted to seek out Alec, so I sit there in silence for a few moments.

Alec breaks the quiet moment by asking, "How are you doing, Willow?"

"I'm fine..." I say, looking down at my hands.

Alec sits up and leans closer to me. He grabs my hands in his and looks me in the eyes. "No you aren't." He pushes my hair from my face and my heart melts in response. My eyes water and I try my best to blink the tears away. "Hey, it's okay, Willow. I know you're strong, but things have to be tough for you right now." He pulls me into a hug.

Being in his arms feels comfortable and normal. Nothing has seemed right these past few days but being in his arms brings back that normalcy I've been craving. I let out a few tears, then take a deep breath and back away. "You're right. Things are kind of messed up right now." I sit back down.

Alec sits at the edge of his bed so that he's still within arm's reach of me. "I know. I'm so sorry. I hate this, Willow! I hate that I wasn't the one to comfort you when you needed me. It's been eating me alive. I am such a fool. I should have understood that you needed to help your parents. I should have trusted that what you felt for me was real. I let the insecurities dig in deep. I..."

I put my hand on his arm to stop him from his deep confessions. Knowing that Alec has been feeling this guilty these past two days hurts. "Don't be sorry Alec. I understand now. I know I lied and I don't know why I didn't trust you or take you along. In a way, I was trying to protect you and there's also something deep down that tells me there was another motive. I'm not in touch with myself enough right now to fully understand that motive but I know that it hurt you. I'm so sorry."

He inches closer to me and puts his hand on my knee. "No, I'm sorry. I shouldn't have broken up with you. Not like that. You just lost your parents and your... your friend." His hand clenches a little but he forces it to relax again. "I was just upset and I didn't really think everything through. I just reacted. When I heard you calling for him in your sleep, I couldn't take it and I snapped. It was wrong."

I look away. What can I say to that? "You weren't wrong. Please don't be sorry," I whisper.

He gently guides my chin with his fingers until I'm facing him again. "Please let me help you. I want to be there for you this time."

A stray tear falls down my cheek and he wipes it away gently. He leans in and places his lips on mine. I close my eyes and try to pretend like I'm back in the shelter. That things are normal and my life isn't broken. That both my parents are still alive.

Without breaking the kiss, Alec pulls me up from the chair and while we're both standing, he pulls me so close to him that we could almost be one. His gentle kiss deepens with an urgency that tells me it's been too long since we've been together. His left hand is warm against my lower back. He runs his right hand through my hair. I hold on tightly to him as I'm swept up in the whirlwind of warmth and safety that he exuberates. I want that safety; I crave that normalcy. If only our kiss could take us back in time to when my life wasn't torn into pieces. If only...The mirage fades away before me as I come to my senses. I put my hand on his chest and pull back, breaking the kiss. I shake my head. "I can't."

Disappointment flashes in his navy eyes. "I shouldn't have done that. I don't know what I was thinking." He runs his hands through his dark hair and stands up. He walks over to the window.

I take a deep breath and then I stand up and join him. This safe house is located right next to the woods and the window in this room looks over a row of tall evergreens.

"It's okay. I just can't do this right now though. Too much has happened. I'm different now. I don't think I will ever be the same." I bite my lower lip. I don't want things to be awkward between us.

He turns around and looks at me. "Don't be sorry, Willow. I just wish I knew what I can do for you."

"You can be my friend. I really need my friends right now." My heart stops in anticipation of what his answer will be. I can tell now that being friends is not what he wanted. He wanted to go back to the way things were. I wish we could but I'm just not the same now.

He puts his palm on my cheek and smiles softly. "We were pretty good friends. I think I can do that." He kisses me on the forehead and drops his hand.

"Thank you," I mouth to him, feeling relieved. Deep down I don't kid myself. I know he may not be satisfied with friendship and perhaps this isn't the last time we will talk about this. For now though, I will accept what I can get, as long as I don't lose Alec too. I need him in my life. My friends mean too much to me. They are like my family.

"Well then, as our first act as friends, maybe we ought to go find Connor and Claire and see if there is any trouble to be found in this hotel." He watches me for a response.

I give him a half smile, which must be satisfactory

enough for him. He grabs my hand and pulls me towards the door. "Maybe we should hold off on the trouble though." I add.

He squeezes my hand, "Deal."

I let him lead me down the hall and up two flights of stairs. We find Connor and Claire in a small room labeled: Recreation Center. Alec opens the door for me and I get a good look at a Ping-Pong table and a pool table before Claire attacks me in a full-fledged hug.

"Willow!" she exclaims. She hugs me tightly and I revel in the comfort my best friend brings me.

I hold on tight. A minute later I feel the wetness soak through the shoulder of my shirt. I pull away from Claire and find her crying. "Claire," I say with worry.

That causes her tears to fall even more freely. She hunches over crying heavily with her hands covering her face. I pull her to me again. Connor looks on worriedly from the corner.

As I hold her, I close my eyes and open my emotions up. I feel Claire's relief that I returned. How much it ate her up inside not knowing if I would make it back alive. I also feel the hurt and her sense of loss. She had grown to love my mom. Everyone dies on her.

"I'm back, Claire. We are all safe now." Although I know one person is excluded. I pull her back so I can see her. I catch the reflection of my black irises through her eyes. "I'm sorry, Claire. I know that you loved my mom."

She looks ashamed and I can feel the emotions as if they were my own. She wipes at her eyes and says, "I just feel like it's wrong for me to feel sad. You are the one who's mourning for your mother. You shouldn't need to comfort me... I have no right to feel this way." She darts her purple eyes away from mine.

I put my hands on her shoulders and shake her lightly. "No, Claire. You have every right to feel sad. I am not the only one who mourns for her. We can remember her together."

Claire looks at me uncertainly and I pull her into another hug. "It's okay. We are going to be okay." I pat her back. Saying those comforting words to my best friend actually allows the words to sink into my heart. As I look around at my friends together in this room, I know that things will be okay. Maybe not right away...but eventually.

Connor comes up behind Claire and wraps his big lanky arms around us. "Group hug!"

That earns a soft giggle from us. Connor is great at breaking tensions, I'm so grateful to have him as a friend. Alec comes and joins in on the hug too and eventually we are a mixture of limbs with Claire and me sandwiched in the middle.

When we break apart, our eyes are dry and our hearts are just a little bit less broken. "We are all together." I look at each of them. "And with that, I have to tell you that I think I'm going to need your help." I hadn't thought of including them before, but these are my friends. What makes me think that they are any less capable of completing a rescue mission than I am? I look at Connor first, "Connor, you still want to find your parents right?" I'm not sure if his parents could be prisoners but one way or another I am determined to help him figure out what happened to them.

He nods his head. "Yes, Lily has been having a hard time adjusting. I need to find them for her."

"We will find them," I tell him. Then I add, "I saw her in the classroom earlier. She was putting a puzzle together."

He smiles proudly. "Yeah, she's a smart cookie. Though the teacher's say she won't let any of the other kids too close to her. She hasn't made any friends here."

"It'll take some time. Reading emotions is a hard ability for a child to possess. However, children are so much more flexible than we are. I think we underestimate just how much they can handle," I tell him.

"That's true." Connor seems as if he hadn't really thought of it that way.

I look to Alec next. "What about your dad?" I can't believe I hadn't thought about his dad before now. He is probably among one of the taken prisoners... that is if he was lucky enough to survive the Reaper attacks.

"I do need to find him. He may have been a Class A Jerk but he's still my dad," Alec says.

A thought occurs to me. The old me would have kept it to myself but the new Willow is determined to be honest with her friends. "Are you prepared to handle it if he was in cahoots with Dr. Hastings?"

Alec's eyes turn dark as he considers it for a moment. He nods, "If that was the choice he made then there will be consequences."

I nod firmly and then address all of them. "If you all are up for it, I would like your help in saving the rest of the prisoners..." I bite my lip. "I have to admit though that I don't know where they are. When we went back after Dr. Hastings, the prisoners had been moved."

Alec looks confused. "You went after Dr. Hastings?"

I realize I hadn't told them where I was going when I left with Tony. I just assumed that my dad would clue them in. I look over at Claire who has a guilty expression on her face.

"You told me that she went to find supplies," Alec addresses Claire.

She avoids eye contact when she says, "I'm so sorry, Alec. You were just so torn up about not being able to help Willow after her mom died..."

I look at Alec in surprise. He quickly averts his gaze from mine but not before I see the truth in them.

Claire continues, "When Willow's dad told me that she went after Dr. Hastings, I knew that it would tear you up inside with worry. I couldn't bring myself to tell you the truth." She looks over at Connor. "I'm sorry, Connor, I shouldn't have lied." Her eyes tear up and I can see the fear in them. She's worried she messed up big time. I can totally understand that feeling since I've for sure been there and done that...more than once.

Connor grabs her hand and squeezes it. "You were just trying to protect your friend. I'm not mad at you. I love you babe." He gives her a light kiss.

Claire turns to Alec. She fidgets with her nails as

she waits for his anger to turn on her. "I'm so sorry, Alec."

When he meets her eyes, he says, "I forgive you. I understand that you were trying to protect me but I want you to be honest with me in the future. I can handle the truth."

Claire nods her head. "Most definitely. I will. I'm sorry again."

Alec gives her a half smile. "I'm not mad at you. I will be if you say you are sorry one more time though." He tries to play off lightening the mood. He turns his attention towards me. "So you went after Dr. Hastings? How did that go?"

My face turns serious as I say soberly, "I killed him." The audible sound of the three of them gasping in unison would almost be funny if it weren't for the situation. "I didn't really have a choice. He was going to kill Tony and it was either his life or Tony's."

"You made the right decision," Claire assures me. The others agree as well, even though I can see the jealousy flash across Alec's eyes.

"What about Zack?" Connor asks.

I shake my head. "He wasn't there so I don't really know."

"So he may not know about his dad? Or who killed him?" Alec asks with worry in his expression.

"I have no idea. It probably won't be long before he finds out that his father is dead. I honestly don't know how he'll react to the news. I do need to find Candy though. Maybe she can help us," I say.

"Yes! Maybe Zack will release the prisoners now that his dad's out of power." Claire sounds idealistic.

I wish I could believe that, but I have a gnawing feeling that Zack may have turned into something even darker than his father. Either way, I need to find him alive so I can find out if he knows a cure that will prevent Tony from turning into a Reaper.

"So how can we help?" Connor asks.

I shrug my shoulders because I don't have a plan yet. "Tony is meeting with Lee and some others. Hopefully, they will work on ironing out a rescue mission. If you are willing to help with it then I know your abilities can be utilized. Are you all in?"

"Yes!" they say in unison.

Connor puts his hand in the middle of our group, waiting for us to place our hands on top of his to do some type of rally chant. We leave him hanging and he sulks while he drops his hand to his side again. Alec gives him a consolatory pat on the back and he lightens up.

"We should go find Candy. Will you go with me, Claire?" I ask, figuring that having her along will help me. I have no idea how Candy will react when I tell her that I killed her father. I try to put myself in her shoes and that makes me cringe. Could I still be friends with someone if they killed one of my parents? Even if my parent was evil? I run my hands over my face. It's like an impossible question in which no answer could exist.

We leave the guys in the rec room and head out in search of Candy.

I have to ask around but eventually we find Candy hanging out in Jake's room. I had nearly forgotten about the beefy blonde boy she met at the bonfire a few nights ago. The door to his room is open and when we approach, we find her sitting next to him laughing. She runs her hand through her long blonde hair. Her baby blue eyes are brightly lit and for the first time in a while, she looks genuinely happy.

I don't want to be the one to take that from her. I consider whether I should just leave and allow her to stay peacefully unaware of her father's death and her brother's crossover into possible evil-dom. She has a right to know, I tell myself. I gather the courage and knock on the door.

Both Candy and Jake turn to look at me. Candy jumps up and comes to my side. "Willow." Her eyes look sympathetic as she asks, "How are you doing?"

It's still so odd to see Candy caring. I know it's the absence of her father's pull that allows her to be free to care about other people. I bite my lip and wonder again if this will be good news or bad. "I'm hanging in there," I say honestly. "Um, can we maybe have a word with you in private?"

Candy looks a bit surprised but only takes a second before she turns around and tells Jake, "I'll be back in just a sec, K?"

"I'll be waiting." He smiles.

Candy giggles and, for once, the sound of her laugh doesn't sound like nails to a chalkboard. It sounds like happiness. My heart starts accelerating and my nerves work in overdrive as I lead her and Claire to my room.

Once the door is closed and we all take a seat, Candy asks, "What's going on?"

"Willow needs to talk to you," Claire tells her.

"Then why are you here?" Candy doesn't sound accusatory, just inquisitive.

As a buffer in case you don't like what you hear, I think. "I asked her to be here for both you and me when we have this talk." I take a deep breath.

Candy's eyes dart between the two of us and she starts clasping and unclasping her hands out of nervousness. "So, this isn't going to be a good talk, is it?"

I shake my head slowly. I really dread what I'm about to tell her. "I know you were at the funeral and you are aware of my mom's death..." I look away and I have to force myself to breathe because just talking about my mom hurts. Especially when I have to use past tense. "Has anyone told you how she died?"

I look up to find Candy's eyes starting to water. She nods her head sadly. "I'm so sorry, Willow. Yes, I know that my father was responsible. I don't know what to say... I'm just so sorry," she says, stuttering while trying to find the right words. She looks at me with worry. It hadn't occurred to me that she could be just as nervous about talking to me about this as I am with her. "My father has a way of taking away the things we care about most." A tear escapes as she recalls her own mother's death.

"I don't blame you at all, Candy, please don't think that." I watch the relief flood across her features. "But, that's not really what I wanted to talk to you about."

Candy straightens up a little and wipes the tear away with the back of her hand. "What do you need to talk about?"

"Tony and I went back to the prison and..." I judge from Candy's expression that she wants me to just get on with it. Say what I came here to say. "We found your father. Some things happened and I didn't have a choice. He was going to kill Tony and I couldn't let that happen..." The lump in my throat makes it almost unbearable to speak the next words. "I feel like you need to hear this from me first..." I look away, not ready to see the judgment in her eyes. "I killed your father."

She gasps and when I force myself to look her in the eyes, she's looking away and her expression is blank. Needing to know her feelings, I open up the part of me that will let them in.

I feel the shock of my words bouncing across her mind like an echo. The mixed emotions of sadness for the loss of the father who gave her life, and relief that he can no longer cause any more pain, tear at her like a rope in tug-o-war. There's an underlining piece in her that feels like her mother has finally been avenged. Then there is a feeling of loss, grief and worry for what her future will be like now that she is parentless.

Her eyes meet mine as she thinks of her brother. Her expression hardens. I know she hates it when I invade her privacy with my gifts, she's told me before. She knows when I do it.

"I'm sorry," I tell her, not needing to be more specific. She already knows that I am. I just need to know now if she hates me.

She forces her to push away the anger that was building because of my intrusion into her private feelings. "What about my brother?"

"He wasn't there," I tell her. "I don't know where he is."

Candy stands up and heads towards the door. "I have to find him. He'll need me."

I jump up from the bed where I'd been sitting. "Wait. There's more..." Candy stops and gives me her attention so I continue. "We are going back for the prisoners. You can come with us, but you need to know that your brother is different."

"What do you mean he's different?" Her blue eyes are open wide.

I don't care for the way she said different either. "I don't know the extent of it, but I believe he was helping your father with whatever plan they were trying to commence. He helped your father take the prisoners."

"My father would have forced him to do that. Now that he's gone, he is free too. He will do the right thing and hand over the prisoners," Candy says assuredly.

Claire chimes in. "Tell her about his eyes," she urges me.

Candy looks at Claire for a moment, and then turns her attention to me in question.

"A lot has changed with your brother. He's not the

same anymore; his eyes are different. He has a lot of colors like mine in them but half of his iris is red." I tell her.

Her lower lip falls open. "Like a Reaper?" she asks.

I nod my head. "He's not full blown Reaper but there is something not right with him. I don't know to what extent he has changed because of these powers, but I don't believe he is on the side of good."

Candy shakes her head in denial. "No, he could be just like you Willow. I don't know how he got all of the colors like you have but that doesn't make him bad. Just like it doesn't make you bad. I mean, you obviously have some red in your eyes too."

Sure I have a speck of red but half of my eye isn't that color, I think to myself but don't say aloud. I want to tell her about my witnessing Zack inject Tony with the red shot. I don't believe that if Zack were like me, he would have knowingly tried to take a person's life like that. Even if it wasn't technically a death shot, he knew what it would turn Tony into. Who knows how many other's he injected with the same thing. The thought sends chills down my spine. I can't tell Candy though. I'm the only one who knows about it. Instead, I say, "Look, you're right. He may have just been under your father's influence. In fact, I would love it if that is the case." Because if he's good, he might tell me how to help Tony. "But you need to go into this with an open mind. You need to be prepared to deal with it if your brother has truly taken a turn for the worse..." I take a step closer to Candy to better illustrate my upcoming question. "Are you ready to deal with that?"

She takes a few moments to question it, biting her lip in thought. I make sure that I don't invade her privacy while she thinks. Finally, she says, "Yes. I'm ready."

"Good. We'll need to meet downstairs in an hour with the others. They're ironing out the details of the mission," I tell her and Claire.

"The mission?" Candy asks.

"To rescue the prisoners," I tell her. Because she's still worried I add, "That is if your brother doesn't automatically release them to us."

She nods stoically.

Claire puts her hand on Candy's back. "Maybe he will. Maybe we will get there and he will have already freed them all." Leave it to Claire to always believe the best in people.

Candy gives Claire an appreciative smile and then leaves the room. I'm glad I brought Claire with me. I honestly wish I could believe that things will end perfectly with one big bright happy ending. But these last few days have taught me that life isn't made up of shiny moments. Life is hard; it's gritty. One day you are filled with joy and the next, you are crawling through the muddy trenches with no inkling of when you might be able to climb your way back up again.

"Thanks for your help," I tell Claire.

"Anytime." She puts her hand around my shoulder knowing that I need the comfort too. "Let's go find our... I mean, the guys."

I nod my head as we leave the room. I wonder how

Claire feels about Alec and me breaking up. Both of us dating best friends was an ideal set up. I can't help but wonder what she thinks of Tony and me.

The guys haven't left the rec room so they are easy to find. Claire kisses Connor immediately when we enter the room. Alec and I both look away at the same time and end up making eye contact. I can see the fire in his eyes that tells me he is not letting go even if I say we need to just be friends.

My cheeks heat and I feign interest in a game on the table. Just like the others in the old safe house, this one is a board game. It's called Trivial Pursuit. Giving Claire and Connor some much-needed privacy, I open the box to look at it closer. I find a bunch of pie shaped wheels and several little colored pie slices that I think are supposed to fill the wheel. I pull out one of the cards from the deck and read it. I've played trivia games like this on my tablet before, but I can't answer this question for the life of me.

I didn't realize Alec had come up behind me until he snatches the card from my fingers and reads it aloud. "Name the phrase coined for the infection a fan obsessed with junior pop artist, Justin Bieber, has."

I look at him like he's crazy. "Who's Justin Bieber?" And how on earth would he infect someone?

Alec shrugs his shoulders. "I have no earthly idea." He turns the card over in his hand to read the answer. "I know it's killing you and you just have to know the answer..." I laugh. He continues, "Bieber Fever."

I shake my head. "That is so... weird." We both

laugh.

To pass the time before our meeting, Alec and I sit down at the table and look through some more of the cards. I can't answer any of them. It seems the one's we keep picking up have to do with entertainment stars or sports stars from the past. We can't help but laugh at all of the silly questions that make no sense. There was one about a pop star who wears a dress made out of raw meat. The answer was Lady Gaga. How absurd! A footnote said she asked someone named Cher to hold her meat purse. I mean, would a purse made of meat really be of any use? Maybe it was made of jerky…

I laugh hard enough that tears come to my eyes. Laughing feels good. It's been a while and it's another thing that gives me the sense of normalcy I've been craving. In my fit of laughter, I hadn't noticed that someone entered the room until Tony comes to stand beside me.

I look up at him and see a mixture of hurt and jealousy in his expression. All humor dies within me melting like snow under a heat lamp. I swallow hard, "Hi, Tony."

He looks from me to Alec and then back at me. "Are you having fun?"

The tone in Tony's words stings and I open my mouth to respond but Alec distracts me by standing up quickly. The sound of his chair screeching against the tile floor hurts my ears.

"Yes, is there a problem with that?" Alec asks with a little too much machismo. I really hope this isn't a pissing contest in the making.

My eyes open wide as I look at Tony's expression. He looks none too happy. He doesn't let it get to him though. Instead, he tries to go the cool route. "No. Willow's happiness is important to me. If she was having fun, then by all means, I don't mean to interrupt."

"Ouch," I think. Tony's eyes dart to mine and I realize he's heard me. "This is not what you think it is."

"What do you think I think it is?" he asks in a tongue-tying thought.

"I don't know. We are just hanging out as friends, nothing more." I don't know why I feel the need to further clarify that. It's not like I'm Tony's girlfriend or anything like that. I don't mention or think about the kiss Alec and I shared. My heart does double time worrying that I've messed up something with Tony... something that isn't even there yet.

"Am I interrupting something?" Alec asks, seemingly annoyed.

I realize that obviously within the time we've been having this inner monologue conversation, it seems like we are just staring at each other in silence.

"No," Tony says quickly. "I was just coming to tell Willow that we're ready for her to come down."

My being around Alec has hurt Tony. I realize this, but he's going to have to find a way to get used to it. Because I plan on keeping my friendship with both of them, no matter what happens. "Okay. I'm ready." I move from the table and realize I need to clue Tony in. "My friends are coming on the mission with us too."

Tony flashes his yellow eyes at me. "Absolutely not!"

"They can help!" I steady my stare, letting him know I'm not going to waver.

"They are a liability! They aren't even trained to fight," he demands.

"They have been training every day since we've come here." He shakes his head and I can see from Alec's expression that he's thoroughly confused by whatever is going down between Tony and me. I finalize my demand by telling Tony, "This isn't up for discussion. They are coming."

Tony turns abruptly and stomps out of the room. Not before throwing one last thought in my direction, "Fine, if they get hurt then it's on you."

Those words pierce the worst. I throw up an invisible wall in my mind so Tony can't hear or feel the hurt. It doesn't matter anyhow because he's already walked out of the room.

Alec puts his hand on my shoulder. "Are you okay?" he asks sincerely.

"Yes," I whisper, not entirely sure that I'm being honest. I don't want to talk about it. "We'd better get down there." Connor and Claire walk up and the four of us head downstairs to the meeting point.

We meet the others downstairs.

It looks as if about twenty or so people are waiting for us. I look around and a lump forms in my throat. Old habits die hard, I realize as I admit to myself I am looking for my mother to start the debriefing. I begin to wonder who's going to be leading the group now that she's gone.

Mr. Leroy stands on a crate and clears his throat to get everyone's attention.

"Thank you all for being here." He looks around the room at each of our faces. "Due to the absence of one of our former leaders, the need has arisen to appoint a new leader for this mission. This person will lead alongside me. Is there anyone here that wishes to nominate someone for this position? Please take into consideration the characteristics this person needs to possess for this role." He takes a dramatic pause looking around the room. His gaze lands on me and stays there for several uncomfortable seconds. "Willow," he says aloud. "I nominate Willow."

My eyes get round as saucers. I can't be a leader! I'm only sixteen! Before I can say 'no', Alec chimes in. "I second that nomination."

Before I can let this sink in, one person after another agrees with Mr. Leroy's nomination. My heart threatens to beat out of my chest. Oh. My. Gosh, I think to myself.

My wall must not have worked well enough because Tony has heard my nervous cries. "Consider it an honor, Willow. If you deny these people what they want, you can expect them to be wary. They need to have the leader they desire. Apparently, that person is you." I didn't even realize he had walked up right next to me. He gives my hand a squeeze of reassurance and lets it go again.

I give him a sideways look. How can Tony go so quickly from cold to hot? Was he not just yelling at me a few minutes ago? Now he thinks I should lead these people... I let out a deep breath. I look around as more people step forward and agree that I should take my mother's place. "Tony, I am only sixteen! I can't do this! Everyone is crazy."

"Josiah became King of Judah at the age of eight. Joan of Arc led the French Army at nineteen. King Tut led all of Egypt at age nine. Age isn't everything you think it is. Your heart and your spirit speak more than a simple candle count on your birthday cake," Tony encourages me.

I give him a sideways glance. Who knew Tony was so passionate about history? Or so good at giving pep talks.

Unable to avoid eye contact any further, Mr. Leroy motions for me to come forward. My feet feel like lead as I move to the front of the room. He puts his arm around me and gives it a squeeze. Normally this would make me extremely uncomfortable, but right now, I feel like he's grounding me to the earth. He leans in and whispers in my ear, "They remember your mother. You are her blood; you were born to lead."

Tears threaten to escape. I feel like her death is so final, like I'm here to take her place. Like she never existed… Tony's right though. If I don't accept, we could fall apart. I am my mother's daughter, I think to myself over and over again.

Tony must hear me because I can see him smiling through the crowd as he says to me, "Yes you are." His smile beams at me. He couldn't be more proud. After all, I am pretty much his protégé. Perhaps this makes up for him being so pissed at me for hanging out with Alec... and the fact that I invited them to come along with us on this mission.

I look around the room at some of the familiar faces and some of those who are still strangers to me. Somewhere deep within, I find the strength. The strength I was born from, that I never knew I possessed. The quiet crowd stands in anticipation, waiting to hear my decision. I take a deep breath, readying myself for something that's about to change my life forever. I swallow hard. "I'm not sure what you all see in me that would consider me leader material. I never thought of myself in this way before. However, I am my mother's daughter; that is something I'm very proud of. It's in her memory that I accept your nomination. I know I'm only sixteen, but I plan on making you proud." I pause, gauging their reactions. The only feeling I get back is pride and loyalty. I turn to Mr. Leroy. "I look forward to leading alongside you." Nods and mumblings of approval emanate from the crowd. "I'd like Tony to be my second in command. My mother appointed him to be my protector and I trust her judgment that he is an integral part of these missions. He's never failed me before." The real reason lies buried deep down inside. I have to keep Tony near me or else... I don't even want to think about it. I can't let him become a Reaper. I care too much for him. I need to be there in case he needs healing.

"Thank you," I hear Tony say, cutting through my thoughts.

I see Alec from across the room and open myself up to his feelings. Jealousy and hurt emanate from him. I don't know if it's from the fact that I'm asking to have Tony work at my side or if it's because he expected me to choose him or something. I feel horrible, but it's what's necessary. I know I've made the best and only decision that makes sense right now.

"Thank you for giving me this opportunity," I say to the crowd. They start clapping and I turn to Mr. Leroy, looking a bit lost. I don't know what to do next.

"We better grab your second in command and go hash out the details." He gestures with his hand for me to lead the way out of the room. The crowd parts for us like the Red Sea and Tony, Mr. Leroy, and I make our way into an adjoining room that has been set up as a command post. I never got the opportunity to see inside the command post when my mother lead. I am quite impressed by the efficiency of the data laid out before us.

Tony closes the door behind him. My heart rate

begins returning to normal, thankful for the retreat from the spotlight. I look around, taking everything in. There are several hand-drawn maps lining the walls. It looks to me like it's the handy work of Tony. I don't even have to ask him if he drew them, he tells me through his thoughts.

A pad of paper sits on the table with several different colored pens to the side. I pick up the paper and immediately recognize my mother's handwriting. I smile at her memory, seeing her doodles on the side margins. I can remember her doing the exact same thing at home. Anytime she would write anything, from a grocery list to a note, it would have doodles in the margins. I trace my fingers over a smiley face she'd drawn. I rip the page out and fold it, putting it in my pocket; filing it with the letter my mother wrote me that I'm too scared to open. Good grief, I think to myself. I'm too chicken to open a letter, but I'm now these people's leader...

Tony chimes in. "You'll do wonderful, Willow."

I smile at him. "Thanks," I say aloud.

Mr. Leroy checks his pockets. "I forgot something. I'll be right back," he says before exiting the room, closing the door snugly behind him.

Tony wastes no time grabbing me and pushing me against the wall. His actions take me completely by surprise and my stomach rolls in a strange excitement. "You have no idea the effect you have on me, Willow," he whispers into my ear. My toes curl at the huskiness in his voice. I wrap my hands around him and hold him tightly to me. There is something different about Tony, he never acts this brusque, but I'm not complaining.

"I'm sorry I reacted the way I did earlier when you were with Alec. It's just… I can't help but feel jealous when I see you with him. Especially since you have a history, a history that is deeper than ours." I feel his breath against my skin in the fold between my shoulder and neck. Goosebumps form along my arms, sending electric tingles running down my legs.

I try to find my voice. Having him this close doesn't help my mind to form clear thoughts. "I accept your apology," I say awkwardly.

"Now that that's out of the way… Do you know how badly I want to kiss you?" he asks me.

I close my eyes reveling in his touch. "Not as badly as I want to kiss you," I say to him in my mind.

He leans back a fraction of an inch so that our noses are touching. His lips are so close, yet too far away. He leans in and our lips meet at the same instant the door handle turns to open.

As quick as lightning, Tony dashes to the other side of the room leaving me breathless and a hot mess. I try to compose myself but to no avail. Tony has an uncanny ability lately to catch me off guard whenever he's near.

I clear my throat as Mr. Leroy enters the room. He must notice my heavy breathing but doesn't mention it. I guess there's some perks about being a leader. He wouldn't question his suspicions… at least not out loud. I don't try to listen to his thoughts because truth be told, I don't really want to know what he's thinking.

Mr. Leroy clears his throat. He reaches for a map and unrolls it on the table. Several dots on it indicate different locations. I run my finger along the circles recognizing the mountain where we used to live, the prison, the safe houses, etc.

"Our informants got back late last night. They were finally able to locate the other prisoners but weren't able to tell us much more about what's going on without putting themselves in danger."

I nod my head. "To be very clear," I say. "Safety of all individuals and soldiers is my number one priority."

Mr. Leroy looks up from the map and nods his head. "It was your mother's too," he says simply.

I give him a small smile that doesn't quite reach my eyes. It's bittersweet hearing of someone else's memories of my mother and the good nature of her personality. I'm honored to be carrying on her legacy.

Mr. Leroy points to a location that doesn't have a marker on it. "This is where they're being held," he says, pulling out a sticker from his pocket. I guess that is what he initially forgot. I hope he forgets something else... He places a sticker on the spot and looks at me again. I take a closer look at the location and see they've been taken to the maze ruins.

"The maze ruins?" I question aloud. I don't even have to wonder why they'd been taken there. It's genius. The maze ruins are an old amusement park that was shut down after multiple people went missing. It's literally a giant maze created from bushes, cornfields, and small buildings.

It's an eerie labyrinth of confusion that was created to be fun. My mother and father took Sabby and me there when we were younger. We had to wear special masks because we were out in public. My mother was getting cabin fever and she insisted we all go on a day trip. What was meant to be an hour-long outing, turned into ten hours of being lost. By the time we found our way out of the maze we were so hungry and above all, tired and relieved. I vowed never to revisit that place. I guess I'll be breaking that promise.

"Willow," Mr. Leroy says. "I must warn you that there is something strange going on right now. When the soldiers got back from staking out the area, they recounted some disturbing details. I want you to know what they are so you'll be prepared to deal with them when the time comes."

I gulp rather loudly and nod my head.

Mr. Leroy walks to the door and opens it a quarter of an inch. "We're ready for her," he says and closes the door.

Not sure what to say to Mr. Leroy, Tony and I wait in silence. "Have you ever been to the maze ruins?" I ask Tony in my mind.

He shakes his head. "They're creepy and I'm really not looking forward to it, that's for sure." He gives me a look of surprise. "You've been there?"

I nod my head. "When I was young," I finish the thought as the door opens. A young woman, who looks to be about my age, enters with a pink scarf around her neck. I notice this first since it's not the least bit cold outside…at least not cold enough for a scarf. She's a few inches shorter than me with strawberry blonde hair. I have to admit that she's very beautiful. It's strange when a small ounce of jealousy runs through me as I hope that Tony doesn't find her as attractive as she obviously is. I push that away, knowing how absurd such a feeling is.

Her eyes dart around the room and she seems on high alert, waiting for something bad to happen. I'm not sure why I do it but I use my power of controlling emotions. I'm sure as rain that my eyes are black right now. I use this power to calm the poor girl. Chances are, if she can chill out, she'll be far more helpful to us. It doesn't take but a second before I see her visibly relax.

She gets further into the room and I notice her eyes are golden. They glimmer in the most interesting way… like they're flecked with pure gold.

My heart begins to race knowing I'm about to receive a new power. I walk over to her and extend my hand. "Hello, my name's Willow. And we're all glad you're here."

She reaches out her hand and hesitantly takes mine in hers. "I'm Marya, it's nice to meet you."

Marya. It's such a unique and beautiful name. I like the way it rolls off my tongue. "Please, have a seat." I pull out a chair for her. She sits down and places her hands in her lap.

"We rescued Marya from the maze ruins. You may notice the scarf she wears around her neck," Mr. Leroy says. Marya's hand instinctively reaches up towards her neck. Tony and I nod our heads. "Marya, would you mind removing the scarf?" Mr. Leroy asks politely.

She hesitates for a moment but then begins loosening the fabric. I inadvertently gasp when the scarf comes off. I place my hand over my mouth, praying I didn't offend her. She stares at the floor in obvious shame. My heart goes out to this dear girl. Her neck is raw and red. Several puncture wounds are spaced about one inch apart around the circumference of her neck.

I kneel down next to her chair and look her in the eye. "Marya, I don't know what happened yet but anyone that can do this to a girl like you ought to have a death sentence. I give you my word we will take care of you and put an end to whoever did this." I know I don't exactly know what happened but rage has already taken over my reasoning.

She gives me a small smile and looks back down at her hands.

"Do you mind if I ask you what power you possess?" I hope she doesn't mind my asking.

"Telekinesis," she says simply. My eyes go round with shock.

I instinctively look up to see what Tony's reaction is. He looks like a deer in headlights. It's most definitely because he knows that now I'm going to have that gift too.

"This should be interesting," I say to myself and Tony. His thoughts come back to me in a jumbled mess. My guess is he's trying to let it sink in. To be able to move objects with my mind has to be the most powerful gift I've seen as of yet. I truly can't fathom it.

I focus my attention back to the girl. "Marya," I say hoping I can get her full attention. She has the information that could make or break our next mission. "Can you tell me what happened to your neck and any other information you feel is important. We're about to send a team that way to try to rescue the other people that you were with. Anything you tell us, no matter how small, may be key to a successful reconnaissance."

She seems to ponder this for a moment before answering. She takes a deep breath and looks me dead straight in the eyes. "My neck is like this because of the collar. All of us had one. They are used to control us and to keep us sedated so we can't use our gifts to escape. I was completely out of it when I was rescued. All I remember was the pain around my neck as they were trying to remove the collar. But even then I couldn't understand the pain." She stops momentarily, gathering her thoughts. "The leader…he's…ruthless. He'll stop at nothing to get what he wants."

I put my hand on hers in a comforting gesture. "Do you know who the leader is and what he or she's after?" I have a horrible suspicion already of course; I just want to hear it come from her.

She purses her lips together looking me dead on. "Power. He wants power. As to who it is, I'm not sure, but they do refer to the person as a 'he'. It doesn't seem like anyone knows his real name. One person will say one name; another one will say a different one. Whoever it is, is after one thing and one thing only... gifts. He wants them all and right now he can't have them all. It's been rumored that there's only one person who can give him what he wants and that person isn't there. That the only reason we were being held captive is to lure that person to him so he can collect what he supposedly deserves."

Mr. Leroy and Tony share a look and then they both turn their attention to me. "You're not going," Tony tells me telepathically.

I stand to my feet. "Darn right I'm going!" I yell a little too loudly. I may be a liability... but I'm the only hope of getting those people out of there. "You see this woman's neck... these people are being treated like barbarians! I can't just sit around on the sidelines twiddling my thumbs while you all risk your lives! None of this would have even happened if it wasn't for me..." My voice gets softer as the guilt sinks in. I hate that so much of this happened because of my accidental injection of the red serum. If I could only go back in time... my thoughts wander. I get up and pace the room trying to sift through this new information. I feel like this is all a big puzzle and we're missing some of the corner pieces. I know she didn't directly say Zack is involved but I'd put money on it! The question is, how in the world does he think I can help him get powers? I think back to his dad asking for my blood in return for my mother's life. The rage starts filling me as I consider the demand. It makes no sense! Zack took my blood back in the shelter and said the tests were inconclusive. What does he expect to find with more of my blood? What would he need with an entire pint of it instead of just a tube or two? I shake my head. Too many questions and nothing adds up. Unless he's just trying to lure me there to kill me since I took his father's life...

Tony starts pacing the room, looking very agitated. I'm sure his mind is considering ways to keep me here, to keep me safe. Mr. Leroy looks back and forth between the two of us. Confusion in his eyes is shortly replaced with a realization that there might be more to our friendship than meets the eye. "Do you mind telling me what's going on between the two of you?"

"Yes, I do!" Tony spins on his heel and directs his frustration at Mr. Leroy. "This mission is too dangerous for Willow. She shouldn't be able to go."

Mr. Leroy seems to ponder it for a moment and for a second I worry that he's going to take Tony's side. Then he says, "We need her on this mission. Her powers are beyond the most powerful weapon we could go into this mission with. Plus, she can flush the leader out if it is in fact her that he wants."

"So you want to use her as bait?" Tony spits, looking none too pleased.

His tone breaks Lee's cool. His face reddens and he opens his mouth. I cut him off before he can give Tony a reprimand for speaking to his superior in such a way. "If I have to dangle myself in the water like a freaking minnow, I will. Those people don't deserve this type of treatment." I point to Marya's neck for emphasis. She looks down timidly and I turn back to Tony. "I will not stand by any longer and let those people suffer because someone thinks I am some freaking key to unlocking a universe of powers."

Its Tony's turn to turn red. He's livid and I can feel it rolling off of him in waves. He doesn't want me to go flitting around in front of Zack, putting my life on the line. "Fine, you want to risk your neck so be it." He stomps out of the room, slamming the door behind him.

I'm left feeling cold and a bit terrified at the upcoming mission. I don't understand how Tony can think that I would just sit down and let other people do the dirty work. Does he not know me? He can't expect me to do anything other than what he would do if he were in my place. I look to Marya, who is still sitting in the chair calmly. The use of my power over her emotions seems to have worked unbelievably well. I wonder how much further I can use the gift. "I apologize that you had to see this. We are going to get the others out, I promise."

She nods her head. "Thank you." She stands up to walk towards the door. "I better get back downstairs. My cousin is waiting for me."

I wonder who her cousin is, but I figure that I will have to get to know her better when this mission is completed. "Thank you for the information," I tell her sincerely.

"Good luck on your mission." She walks to the door and pauses for a moment staring at the closed door. Without reaching for the knob, the door swings open.

I look to Lee with surprise. He nods his head. "It's a powerful gift," he says.

"It sure is." I think of how many times I used to lie in bed not wanting to get up to grab my tablet or the remote control. How I'd think how cool it would be to be able to just make it come to me with my mind. How completely odd it is that now someone can actually do that. And I will be able to do it soon as well.

"How did they get the collar off her?" I ask Mr. Leroy.

"It was actually her cousin who did it. He's one of our guys. When he saw her, he refused to leave without saving her. He found a button on the back of the collar. It came off as easily as pushing the button. The problem is though, that the people wearing it are either too medicated or they are being controlled in some way that makes it to where they don't even think about taking the thing off," he answers.

Wow, I'm amazed that the solution to removing such an atrocity would be a single button release lever. I assumed it would have been something tricky or nearly impossible to remove. That tells me how much control the medication or mind control has over the prisoners. "We need to make sure everyone else knows about this button so we are prepared to save the others."

"The teams are being briefed on it as we speak," Lee says. "We better get down there and join the others."

I follow him downstairs. In the briefing, we discuss team assignments and the general layout of the facility; although we don't know the exact layout of the maze itself, I hope I will remember some details from the past when

I enter it. After more discussion and planning, we head to the cafeteria for dinner. Personally, I wish we would leave for the mission tonight. The others who had done the reconnaissance urged us to leave at first light tomorrow. They said that the maze ruins are not well lit and a nighttime mission would probably leave us at a greater disadvantage.

I eat dinner with my friends, sans Tony. I'm not sure where he stomped off to. He wasn't even at the meeting. After dinner, I stop in to my dad's room and spend an hour with Sebastian and him. I read Sabby a story and then kiss them goodnight. I can feel the nerves rolling off my dad about my upcoming mission. I do my best to assure him that all will turn out alright. Then I head to my room.

I fall asleep as soon as my head hits the pillow.

TEN

The next morning I'm jostled from my sleep by a soft rapping on the door.

Half asleep, I roll over and pull the covers over my head. "One more hour," I mumble to whoever is trying to interrupt my beauty sleep.

A few more seconds pass and another knock raps on the door. I grumble under my breath. It feels like it's still dark outside... at least light isn't coming in through the windows. "What is it?" I say loud enough that the person on the other side of the door can hear me. Not that I really want to hear what they have to say at this ungodly hour.

The door creaks open and then closes. I hear footsteps heading to my bed and immediately I can tell it's Tony. "Good morning, sunshine," he tells me in my head.

I grumble some more under my breath and pull the covers down from my head. He brushes some of the hair away from my face with the tips of his fingers. I melt inside just a little at his touch.

"We need to get up and get breakfast if we want to make good time out of here," he says to me. I rub my eyes trying to wake up. I hate mornings. Tony smiles at my obvious sleepy attitude. "I'll give you a few minutes to get ready," he says. "Meet me downstairs in ten?"

I nod my head. He lightly kisses my forehead and then leaves the room.

As soon as I hear the door catch, I place my hand on the spot where he placed his lips. It might just be my imagination but it feels warm and tingly. Somewhere deep inside I kind of wish it wasn't my head he kissed... What I still can't understand though is how Tony can switch gears so fast. Yesterday he stormed away and didn't even show up to dinner. Then this morning he's all lovey-dovey? His hot and cold mood swings are giving me whiplash. I can't help but wonder if any of this has to do with the change that's coming.

I roll out of bed and stumble around getting ready, still half asleep. I put my hair up in a messy bun and brush my teeth. That's about all I feel up to doing so I head downstairs.

I find Claire on the way downstairs and she waits for me. "Mornin', Claire Bear," I say.

She snickers. "Mornin' yourself. Sleep okay?"

I nod my head. "Slept like a rock." We continue the small talk until we reach the dining hall. Tony, Connor, and Alec wave us over to a table in the far corner. Seeing Tony with Alec seems bizarre but gives me a small inkling of hope that maybe, just maybe, we could all be friends. Candy joins us with Jake a few moments later and we end up having to pull a few more chairs up. Jokes and laughter fill the room as we act our age. It feels nice to act carefree and enjoy my friends, even if for only a little while.

Tony is the first one done. He tells me he needs to go take care of a few things before we leave and asks me to meet him at the Command Post when I'm finished eating. He gives my shoulder a squeeze and leaves.

I can't help but feel the jealousy emanating from Alec. I brush it off and give him a smile. Breakfast this morning was fun and light. There's no need to make it more complicated. I know things are awkward right now. Perhaps if I just came out and said that I think I may be falling for Tony, it would add some closure. I just don't feel as though I can break that kind of news to Alec just yet. I mean, it's only been a few days. Can those types of feelings truly build in such a short period of time? I may have had to grow up rather quickly, but I'm still extremely immature in the love department. I will always love Alec though, that will never change. I don't want him to hurt. A small part deep inside me also tells me that I don't necessarily want to close that chapter just yet, even though I know it's for the best.

By the time I leave breakfast, my sides hurt from laughing so much. Connor was laughing so hard his drink came out of his nose, landing on Claire's food. The look she gave Connor was priceless! Leave it to Connor to provide the comedic relief. I give everyone a hug before I leave, just in case I don't get an opportunity to before we all head out on the mission. Alec's hug seems to last a bit longer than the others, but maybe it's just me.

I stop by my dad's room. Sabby and him haven't woken up for the day. I tiptoe in and give each of them a kiss on the forehead. I whisper, "I love you," before leaving the room again.

I meet Mr. Leroy and Tony in the makeshift command center. They are going over some more hand drawn maps. We further lay out our plans. We will have two different teams going in and another team will stay along the perimeter. One will start at the end of the maze and the other team will start at the beginning. The goal will be to find Zack and trap him in the middle. We will have to contain him until Candy can get there. We are hoping she will be able to get through to him. She still believes there is good in him. I can only hope that she's right, but chances are she's not. I'd like to give her the benefit of the doubt, even when it seems senseless.

After we plan some of the more grueling details, we head out into the conference room. The room is full to the brim with at least a hundred people. Unlike times in the past, I am not looking out at a sea of only yellow eyes. Instead, there are a myriad of different shades present. Everyone is talking amongst themselves but once Mr. Leroy and I stand up at the podium, they quiet down.

"We want to thank you all in advance for being here. This won't be an easy mission and the number of volunteers for this particular one is phenomenal. We will be going over team assignments first, and then you will break away with your team leaders, who will outfit you with the appropriate gear and weapons. Our goal is to run this mission so smoothly that no lives will be lost..." Mr. Leroy continues hashing out the plan and calling out assignments. Since Tony refuses to be on a different team than me, he announces that Tom will be leading the third team who will be patrolling the perimeter. Knowing the details of the mission, I take the time to memorize each person's face. I heed the fact that these soldier's lives will be partially my responsibility. I refuse to take that responsibility lightly.

I don't realize Mr. Leroy has finished talking until all eyes turn on me.

"Willow, would you like to add anything?" Lee asks me.

I wasn't aware that I'd be talking. I feel ill prepared. I stand up anyway and take his place in front of the podium. "Thank you, Lee..." At first, I'm not sure what to say, but then it hits me. I swallow back the emotion that threatens to overcome me. "Seeing all of you, who have volunteered to go on this mission, it's quite moving. We all know how dangerous this undertaking is. Some of you have friends and family who are being held prisoner that you want to save. Some of you don't know anyone in there but you are going on this mission to save the lives of strangers because it's the right thing to do. Every one of you has counted the cost and realizes that this assignment is going to be tough and that it could cost you your life, yet you still stand with us. When I look out at this sea of dedicated soldiers, I can't help but feel the pride that my mom must have felt each time she stood before you. I know that had she been here today, she would be immensely proud, just as I am. Thank you for your service."

I hadn't realized that I closed my eyes the second I brought up my mom. I open my eyes to see several tear-filled ones staring back at me. Then everyone starts clapping and cheering each other on. I smile and step away from the podium.

Mr. Leroy's face is filled with pride and before he steps back up, he quiets the crowd. "Thank you, Willow, for those moving thoughts. I know that your mother would be very proud of you as well." He looks to me and I have to force the tears back to keep them from falling. He turns to address the soldiers. "Please regroup with your designated leaders now. You are dismissed."

Everyone starts walking this way and that. Tony and I head to the far corner of the room where our team has planned to meet. My friends, including Candy and Jake, are on my team as well as another thirty soldiers. We will be going into the maze ruins at the beginning. I lay out some directives and plans. Due to the number of turn offs in the maze, we will be taking each twist in groups of three. I break them all off, making sure I have at least one person with strength for each group. Tony had asked at the beginning for Alec to be assigned to the two of us. At first I didn't like the idea, as I wasn't sure if it would complicate matters. Tony makes a good point though; we need a strong healer with us in case anything happens. I essentially could be using so many other powers that having to fully heal someone who is critically injured would take too much from me. I also justify to myself that not only will I be able to make sure Alec stays safe, perhaps Alec can help me if anything goes wrong with Tony. Maybe the two of us healing him at the same time will have a greater effect of keeping him from turning into a Reaper. I don't want to tell Alec about any of this unless absolutely necessary so I keep the idea in my head... where it belongs. Tony hasn't had any relapses in the past twenty-four hours. Maybe my healing back at the cabin worked. Deep down inside though, I don't believe it.

I go over with the team once again on how to remove the collars; then Tony works on handing out weapons and supplies. Once everyone is comfortable with their weapons and the action plan, we meet with the other teams outside.

We convene once more as a whole and go over the details one last time. You can never be too prepared on an action plan. Then we head out.

The trip to the maze ruins takes around three hours. Throughout the trip we have to not only be aware of any of Zack's soldiers, but we also have to watch out for Reapers. Like before, we run into no signs of Reapers. If there are any out there, I doubt they would attempt to take on a group of our size anyhow, unless they had enough of them to actually do some damage, which is doubtful.

When we reach the point in which the land slopes downwards into a valley, we see our first glimpse of the maze ruins. It doesn't look anything like I remember. The once brightly painted buildings are now faded and years of inattention have caused them to dilapidate. Now they just look eerie and sad. The cornhusks are surprisingly quite tall. The land was still being used to process corn for cattle feed even when the amusement park was closed down. We are too far off to fully judge, but I can only guess that the husks will reach well above our heads. They are no longer green and full of life though, they are dried and brown, far past the time of harvest. The rows of thorny bushes still seem to be in decent shape as they are the only things looking lively down there.

I stand up on my tiptoes even though it does no good. If only we were higher up. Then perhaps I could visually see the correct route through the maze. I guess it doesn't really matter anyway, since our goal is to find each prisoner and, technically, they could be held anywhere throughout the twists and turns.

"Creepy looking, huh?" Alec asks from close behind me.

I nod my head and then turn to him with my finger over my lips. He's obviously had a momentary lapse in memory and forgotten our total silence rule. We need the best advantage we can get. It's awkward not having spoken for so long so I smile, making light of his slip-up.

He sticks his tongue out at me, which makes my smile that much brighter. I catch Tony looking at us from the side and I quickly avert my gaze and focus on the task at hand.

Before making our way down into the valley, we implement the next part of the plan. Every person who can turn invisible is called to action. Surprisingly, those with this power make up nearly one third of our people. Other than those with yellow eyes, they are the next majority in our group.

The people with this skill make their way to the outside of each team. The rest of us are to hold onto them and allow them to keep us invisible until we are at our points of entry. The people on the outside perimeter duty will remain invisible for as long as possible unless they are able to find places to hide. I grab onto Claire's arm. I give Tony a funny look as I do. I wanted to offer my use of the power but once again, Tony thinks it's best that I save my strength. I hate it when he has to make sense.

Together as one large, invisible army, we make our way down through the valley. It only takes twenty minutes for us to reach the outside of the maze. As instructed prior, my group separates from the others. We head to the front entrance. When we get there, I look up at the old sign that states: Maze Ruins- Enter If You Dare. Someone came back with a can of red spray paint and covered the sign with the word CLOSED. The paint has faded to a salmon pink color and looks oddly childlike.

A creepy looking clown face that's weathered from the elements looks down at us as we reach the front gate. A shiver runs up my spine; I've always hated clowns. A rusted chain and padlock keep trespassers out. I wonder how Zack got everyone in so easily without breaking the padlock. I let go of Claire, becoming the first person visible. I feel slightly vulnerable. Tony is at my side, out in the open, before I know it though. We inspect the lock and sure enough, the lock has been cut. Zack, or whoever else, must have put it back up just for appearances. We pull it off and do our best to remove the chain quietly. The clanking sounds make me cringe and I half expect an army to come running out from around the corner. Eventually we're able to get it off.

Seamlessly and without any words, we break apart into our groups. Those that have a person who can use invisibility stay connected. They will have better chances of not being seen that way. Since those teams don't have healers, that's their best line of defense.

Tony walks to my left and Alec to my right. All three of us have our pistols drawn and ready. We take the first split off. I vaguely remember this being one of the correct ways to go. It was so long ago that I was here last but I chose this route for us anyhow.

My hand shakes a little with nerves as we come upon the first rows of dried, dead corn. I was right that it does reach up over our heads. It looms over us, caging us in to the left and the right. I wonder how this plays in with Tony's claustrophobia. It can't be pleasant for him. I squeeze his hand and he squeezes back, letting me know he's dealing with it the best he can.

So much of the corn is starting to break down, that every once in a while I can look through it and into another row of the maze. That's when I see my first glimpse of bright red hair blowing gently in the wind. I can't see entirely through the husks, but I can tell that the person is lying on the ground and barely moving.

Without thinking, I grab both Tony and Alec's

hands and pull them through the corn, using my powers. I'm sure we could have just hacked our way through the dead sea of husks, but this way is faster and much more quiet.

"Is she…?" My heart starts accelerating.

"No, I think she's still breathing," he assures me. We run to her. She's lying on her side and her long red hair is covering her back.

I bend down to where I can see her face. Her eyes are open but her expression is vacant. Nausea rolls in my stomach and my chest tightens up as I see the collar first hand. It's black with small, clear vial studs in quarter inch increments all around it. Inside the see through vials, you can see a substance that's looks clear like water. This one is running low but the liquid is still noticeable. I've never seen anything so horrendously clever in all of my life. A neck collar filled with needles, how could anyone make something like this?

I force myself to look away as Tony and Alec work on finding the button to remove the collar. I look into the woman's vacant eyes. They are a unique shade of grey. Unlike most grey eyes that can be almost another form of blue, these have no blue tint in them. They are a perfectly stunning shade of grey with a hint of metallic silver around the edges.

I hear the grotesque sound of each vial losing suction as they remove the collar slowly.

"Carefully," Tony tells Alec as he starts removing his side. Alec looks down at the needles protruding. There are four small needles for each vial. He nods his head realizing that Tony means for Alec to be careful to not prick himself with one.

It takes them about a minute to successfully remove the entire collar. Much like Marya, this woman's neck is covered in red splotches. The part where each vial sat is bruised as if the collar was pulled way too tightly against her skin. Alec places his hands on the woman's neck. I watch him as he concentrates on healing her. I realize that I've never really watched Alec using his powers. It's amazing the concentration and dedication that flashes across his features as he focuses all he can on helping this woman. I begin to wonder if that's how I look when I heal. After a few seconds, Alec sways a little. I grab ahold of his arm to keep him steady. His eyes look a little glassy. He removes his hand from the woman's neck and takes some deep breaths.

"Are you okay?" I whisper worriedly.

He takes a second before nodding. Then he shakes his head as if to clear his mind. "It's weird, it's like I could feel some of the effects of the drugs as I was healing her."

I know personally that at times when I've healed people, especially when they are close to death, I have felt the smallest portion of the pain that I assume they must have been feeling. I don't know if it goes hand and hand with the gift or not. It's usually only in the most extreme cases. "Those drugs must be very powerful." I put my hand on his leg.

He runs his hands through his hair and then

notices my hand on his thigh. I focus on giving him some strength. He notices my eyes turn navy. "You need to save your strength."

"Not at the detriment of your safety," I tell him quietly. I'm not going to just sit around and let him turn all loopy every time he helps someone. Alec and I exchange a long, silent stare until Tony interrupts us.

"She's coming to," Tony tells me.

I look back at her and find her stirring. Tony helps the woman sit up. I move from Alec's side so that I can be right in front of her. I look into her eyes. "Are you okay?" It's a silly question and I realize it only after I've already asked it. Of course she's not okay. Her eyes go wide and she doesn't answer me. "We are here to help you. You're safe now." She starts looking around wildly. I grab her chin and force her to look into my eyes. "You will calm down and follow our orders. We are going to get you out of here. Do you know who put you here?"

Her eyes don't glaze over as they should when I use compulsion. Instead, she looks much more freaked out. She jerks her head out of my grip and I look at her stunned. I was able to fend off some of Zack's compulsion back when he used it. I assumed that was because I had the same gift and I was able to manipulate it in a way to make sure it didn't fully work on me. But her eyes aren't hazel like that of someone who can use compulsion.

I try to open up my mind to hear what she's thinking. Tony eyes me when he sees my eyes turn green. I don't hear anything though. It's like her mind is completely clear of all thoughts. I try to feel her emotions and I feel nothing. Nothing is working on her. How bizarre.

Tony takes over in trying to calm the woman down now that she's looking at me like I'm completely nuts. "We aren't going to hurt you. If you want us to help you get out of here alive, you will have to follow our directions. Do you want to?" He adds again, "Get out of here alive?"

She thinks about it for a second before nodding her head. Finally, she speaks and her voice is hoarse. "Yes."

"What's your name?" he asks.

"Jennifer," she says.

"Okay, Jennifer. I'm Tony, this is Alec, and this is Willow. We are all going to help get you out of here. First, is there anything you can tell me about why you are here, why they put those collars on you?" he asks.

"No, we don't know anything. We just know that the one who did this is looking for someone," she says.

My stomach flips and my hands shake.

Tony's eyes find mine before he continues. "Okay, thank you. You are safe. When we run into another group, we will hand you off to them and they will get you out of here. For the meantime, stay close to us." We all stand up. Tony holds out his hand and helps her to her feet.

Curiosity has me asking the next question. "What powers do you have?"

She gives me a look that tells me she doesn't trust me. Then she shakes her head. "I don't know. I saw the ones who had... special abilities, out at the mountain. Then when those men took me to the prison with the others they pulled me aside and questioned me. They kept trying to get me to tell them what I could do, what my powers were. I don't know what powers they are talking about."

"Have your eyes always been grey then?" I ask.

Her eyes bug open and her hands instinctually reach up to her eyes. Great, I freaked her out. Tony steps in and puts his hand on her shoulder. "It'll be okay. Don't worry about it. We have all had changes in our eye color. We will look into it further when we are all out of here safe. Okay?"

She looks torn between wanting to comply and listen to Tony and wanting to run far away from us freaks. She finally nods.

We take that as a cue to start moving again. Thankfully, we haven't run into any guards even though it seems like we were there helping this woman for several minutes.

We walk down the new row of dead corn. I draw my pistol back out as I hear someone around the corner. I turn to Jennifer with my finger over my mouth, telling her to stay silent. She nods and then I turn myself invisible. I take a chance by peeking around the corner. I let out a sigh of relief and let go of my invisibility when I see another one of our teams. I gesture them to us. This team is invisible, but I can still see them.

I whisper to them, "I've found someone. You need to get her out of here. Will you take her out to the team on the perimeter before you continue your search?"

"Yes ma'am," a guy with yellow eyes says.

"Do you remember your way back?" I ask them.

"Yes ma'am," he says.

"Good," I say. I turn to find Tony at my side. "You talk to her," I tell him, since Jennifer obviously warmed up to him a lot more than me. I don't know the best way to tell her that she's going to need to trust some people she can't see. I wonder if their gift of invisibility will even work. I think about Alec healing her. That worked, yet nothing I tried did. How weird.

I overhear Tony whispering to her, "You can trust these people. I know that you can't see them but if you can trust them, they can turn you invisible so nobody can see you. They can get you out of here."

Jennifer looks around and doesn't see anyone. I can tell by her expressions that she's freaking out.

"Can you let her see you?" I ask the team.

They let go of their invisibility, and when Jennifer spots them, her eyes widen. Then realization sets in and she says to Tony, "Thank you. I'll go with them."

"Good. They'll keep you safe," he tells her.

She walks towards the group. An older woman with purple eyes smiles sweetly and then holds her hand out. Jennifer accepts it. I watch as they slowly turn invisible.

I can see them all as usual, so when Tony says aloud, "It's not working. She's not turning invisible." I realize it didn't work.

I think about it for a moment. How was Alec able to use his gift? Then I walk up to Jennifer. I tell her, "I know you have no reason to trust me. But, if you can just trust these people, they can help get you out of here. If they can turn you invisible it would be much easier to get you to safety. I think though, that something is keeping you from allowing their gifts to work. I think it's a matter of trust. You have to open up and trust them."

Jennifer looks from me to the older woman at her side. She closes her eyes and takes a few deep breaths. I watch as her eyes open and she looks down and examines her hands and then her arms. Her eyes are wide with awe.

Tony tells me, "It worked. Good job, Willow."

"No, you did a great job calming her down. Thank you, Tony. I don't know what I'd do without you."

He gives me a smoldering look that tells me he feels the same way towards me.

Alec is standing to my other side. He gives me a strange look. I'm sure Tony and my awkward silences must seem extremely weird since he doesn't know we talk to each other with our minds. The three of us turn our attention to the team as they leave. Then we start moving again.

After one more row of dead corn, we land in the overgrown thorny bushes. I remember hating this section when I was younger. If you lean into them, the thorns prick your skin all over. It's quite uncomfortable. I wonder if I imagined that they were worse than they truly are when I was a kid. I reach my hand out and touch a leaf. "Ouch!" I yell in my head. I examine my finger. There is a pinprick of blood. Yeah, I still hate these things, I think to myself as I put my finger in my mouth.

Unlike the openings in the rows of corn, these

overgrown prickly bushes provide no visibility through them. We make our way quietly down one row and come to a fork in the path. I go with my gut and decide to take the left trail. I assume it would be the best path to lead towards the center of the maze. We start walking and, up ahead, I catch a glimpse of another one of our groups. They are huddled at the end of the row around a figure on the ground.

"They must have found another one," Alec whispers. He starts moving quickly towards them since now we can tell that this is Connor and Claire's group. They are teamed up with Josh, the guy who I tricked into telling me where the prison was.

"We pulled him from the bushes," Claire tells me when I reach them.

I look down to see a boy around thirteen or so lying on the ground looking dazed. His eyes are the same color gold as Marya's are. The collar is already off of him. His neck looks worse than Jennifer's. I wonder if he had an allergic reaction to something on the collar, or in the medication, because his face and neck all the way down to his arms is covered in a light red rash. I kneel down to inspect it further and realize that it's not a rash. There are dozens of small scrapes and cuts, probably from the bushes.

Anger at whoever would do this to a kid starts to ebb away at my calm. "Can you help him?" I ask Alec.

Alec nods his head. Not concerned at all about what happened a few minutes ago when he healed Jennifer, he places his hands over the boy's neck. I watch as the tiny scrapes heal up. When the little puncture marks start closing and fading slightly, I put my hand on Alec's shoulder.

"I think he's good, you can stop," I tell him.

Alec lets go. "I didn't feel the same thing this time. It was there in the background but it was nowhere near as strong as with the girl."

That's strange, but a good strange. I'm glad it didn't affect Alec the same way.

We wait for a moment until the boy starts coming to. Like Jennifer, he starts freaking out. He scoots back from us so fast that we can't stop him from running his back into the bushes. He winces in pain and has no choice but to move forward again. Although there is the worry inside me that says he won't be susceptible to my powers, I still attempt to help him. First, I use my emotion ability to make him feel calm. He noticeably relaxes.

I let out the breath I'd been holding and move towards him so that he can see my eyes. I use my compulsion. "You are safe. We are going to help you. What's your name?"

"John," he says as his eyes glaze over, submitting to my abilities.

"Nice to meet you, John. I'm Willow. These are my friends." I gesture behind me. "We're going to get you out of here. First, can you tell me anything about why you're here? Do you know who did this to you?"

"I don't know who did this. I was with the others in the building. Then early this morning some guy came in looking all pissed off. He looked at all of our eyes and then singled me out. He jerked me up and put the collar on so fast that I didn't know what to do. He dragged me out here and left me. I thought I was going to get away. Then something started stabbing at my neck. I felt sick and fell into the bushes. That was the last thing I remembered."

"Why would they have dragged him all the way out here though?" I wonder.

"Bait," Tony says.

I ignore him because I know he's right. "I'm sorry that this has happened to you, John. What about the others? You said you were in the building with the others."

John nods his head. "Yes, there are a lot of us; in a building somewhere down there." He points towards the middle of the maze where the old buildings are incorporated.

"Are they all in one room? Are they being medicated?" I ask, hoping he can answer the question.

"Yes, we were all in a large room. I was pretty out of it back there so I assume everyone was. It wasn't as bad as when he put that collar on me. That was crazy. At least with the other stuff I still knew I existed. Out here, I thought I was lost forever. I was sure I was as good as dead," he answers honestly. The calming sensation I washed over him must be working because nobody who went through something like this would be able to answer without totally losing it. I personally want to lose it just hearing what happened to him.

"Thank you. Your information has been very helpful," I tell him. "We are going to get you to safety now." I reach my hand out and help the boy up.

I ask Josh, Connor, and Claire to get him to the

team on the perimeter. They don't seem happy about my orders, but I don't care. Part of me knows that things are about to get really bad, really quick. I can't help but feeling better, knowing some of my friends are outside of this maze. I give Connor and Claire a hug before they head out with Josh and John in tow.

When we're alone again, with only Tony and Alec, we start moving.

"Do you find it strange that we haven't run into a single guard?" Alec wonders aloud.

"Yes, it is odd. I don't like it," Tony says eyeing me out of the corner of his eye. "What I really don't like is the convenience we've had in saving both Jennifer and John. Also, I don't think it's a coincidence that last night Marya was rescued and this morning they replace her with someone that has the same eye color."

Ice runs up my spine. "I thought of that too." I just wished I knew exactly why. For what purpose... none of this makes much sense. I get the sneaking suspicion though that it will all add up to some huge diabolical plan. The key is to crack the code before Zack, or whoever's in charge, figures out we know.

We keep walking, following the row of bushes. We make a few turns and, eventually, I see the dilapidated buildings come into view. The windows of the old buildings have been broken out here and there. The paint is peeling and some boards are hanging by their last nail. We walk out of the row of bushes into a large open space. Nobody is in sight! This is absolutely not right.

Tony puts his arm out, keeping me from walking further. We stop and listen. I hear a high-pitch scream coming from inside the building and start running.

"Wait!" Tony yells after me. I can hear him on my heels. I turn to see him next to me. Alec is way far behind without the strength of speed on his side. I consider stopping but then Candy, Jake, and another guy with purple eyes step out from the bushes. He'll be safe with them. At least he's not alone.

Without pausing, I run into the first building to my right. That's where I assume the scream came from. I stop cold when I am faced with nothing but mirrors. There has to be hundreds of mirrors lining the room and they create hallways that lead this way and that. I feel disoriented when I see my reflection and Tony's shooting up all around us. I sway a little and I watch a dozen of Tony's arms reach out to help steady all of the reflected versions of me. I close my eyes to make the sensation that this room is causing cease. I totally forgot about this room. When I was here last with my family, it was one of the funnier moments. Since Sabby was still a baby, he laughed his little cheeks off when he saw himself in all of the mirrors. It was so freaking adorable… nothing like this time.

I open my eyes and look around again. Some of the mirrors are cracked or all out broken. I try to make my way from broken mirror to broken mirror since it helps me get reoriented. I allow myself a moment at each to stare at the empty black frames. Shattered mirror pieces are scattered about on the floor.

I hear another scream so I start running again.

"You can't just run in there blind. Slow down!" Tony yells inside my head.

I don't answer. I keep running. I crash into a mirror. I hear it break apart into a million little pieces. The slicing pain doesn't hit me until a second later. I grab at my forehead and my hand comes away covered in blood. I look into an adjoining mirror and see the blood pouring off my forehead and down the side of my face. There is so much blood in the many reflections of myself that it makes me woozy.

I see Tony coming up behind me in the reflection of the mirror. He's looking down and I wonder if he's hurt. Then I hear, "Did you hurt yourself, sugar?" He looks up and my stomach lurches when I see a dozen pairs of red eyes staring back at me.

My heart works double time and I turn around so fast that it makes me dizzy. The real Tony isn't there; instead, I am faced with another mirror. I catch my reflection in it and see that he's still behind me. I turn again and reach out to the mirror to feel its cold surface; he's not there. I'm totally freaking out when I turn around again and again, not finding the real Tony, just his reflection. I end up turning so quickly that I can no longer keep my balance and I fall to the ground.

My hands get sliced apart against the shattered mirror pieces. I back away with my feet and hands, not caring about the cuts. I look around for Tony, who I can't see in the mirrors anymore. That's when I finally hear the crunch of glass under foot. With the dizzy sensation abated, I stand up quickly. I move backwards until I finally feel a mirror against my back. At least he can't sneak up on me.

I wait until I hear the crunching sound again. Then his laugh sets my blood boiling. I wait until he steps out into view before my suspicions are confirmed.

"Hello, sugar." Zack stares at me with evil eyes. The colors of his eyes are no longer the vibrant mixture of colors they once were. Instead, they are mostly hazel with a small fading trace of the other colors, including the red.

I look at him incredulously. "Your eyes." Of all of the things I could say... that I wanted to say! Instead, I say that?

He laughs evilly. "Yes, my eyes are... fading. Aren't they?" His expression turns angry. "Thanks to you," he spits.

My eyes open wide. "What do I have to do with your eyes?" I ask.

"Wouldn't you like to know? Tell me this, Willow; do you think you're better than me because of all of the gifts you possess?"

I raise my eyebrow. My heart is beating so loudly, I worry it might stop cold from the pressure. "No, I don't, Zack."

He stares at me for several seconds. He opens his mouth to respond but the sound of Candy calling him stops him.

"Zack!" She runs into a few mirrors as she makes her way to where we are. "Zack, you're okay," she says with relief.

"He's dangerous, Candy!" I warn her as she reaches his side.

She rolls her eyes at me and grabs her brother's arm. He faces her and gives her a fake smile. "Sister."

"He's gone, Zack. We can go now. He has no control over us any longer," she urges him, obviously talking about her dad.

Zack's expression hardens, "Yes, he's gone." He turns to me and adds, "Willow murdered him."

Candy looks taken aback. Not by his proclamation since she knows I killed her dad, but by the fact that Zack seems mad about it. "You hated him." She jerks at Zack's hand forcing him to look at her.

Zack looks at her like she's a stupid child. "Yes, but he owed me! He was supposed to give me the powers I deserve. Now he's gone because of her," he says so harshly that I can see the spit spray from his mouth.

I watch Candy wipe at her face with a gross expression. "Who cares about powers, Zack? We don't have to do anything for him anymore. He killed our mom; he deserved to die."

"Does it look like I care about that, Candy? It's not my fault that mom wasn't strong enough to withstand the immunization. It should have made her strong but she was just too weak," he says coldly.

Candy looks like a puppy that's been kicked. It takes her only a second to truly understand how cold and lost her brother is. When she does, she surprises us all. She makes a fist, cocks her elbow back, and punches him square in the jaw with all her strength. "You bastard! You don't talk about our mom like that!" she cries out.

Zack wipes his hair out of his face and then he backhands his sister so hard that it sends her flying back into the mirrors. The glass crashes down around her. Jake and Alec finally find us and they both go running to her side to help her.

Zack turns his anger and wrath on me. "You're coming with me. You're now the only person who can give me what I need."

"I'm not going anywhere with you," I yell at him furiously. I watch Alec from the corner of my eye, working on healing Candy. The glass has cut her badly. I look around wondering where Tony is.

"Yes you are." He snaps his fingers and two Reapers come out from hiding. They start to approach me. "I need your blood," he yells at me.

"What do you need with my blood?" I yell back at him. "Have you turned into a sparkly vampire overnight or something?"

He holds his hands up to keep the Reapers from advancing. I forgot Zack's flair for the melodramatic. He likes to make a scene, so asking him such a question allows him to play his cards perfectly, which in turn, buys me some time. He says, "I still don't know what makes you so special that you get to have all of the powers. I told you that your blood tests back in the shelter were inconclusive and they were... in a way. You see, Willow, while I can't figure out how to recreate a shot that will allow me to have your abilities, I can inject your blood into my bloodstream to get similar results. See the problem is the results faded after a while. Father was supposed to find another way to make it permanent. We considered a blood transfusion but we don't know if that would be a permanent fix. For the mean time, I think having regular injections will have to do."

My stomach turns so badly that I end up vomiting up my breakfast. Zack laughs as I stand doubled over, heaving out the contents of my stomach. He is injecting my blood into him? The thought of it is so incredulous and so grotesquely ridiculous that it makes my stomach roll. I quickly stand back up. He looks at me with an expression of pure delight. My reaction was all that he could have hoped for. I look up and spit towards him. He doesn't flinch. I yell, "You are sick and twisted!"

He smiles as if I've just given him a compliment, "Yes I am."

I notice then that another Reaper has approached Candy, Jake, and Alec. He holds a gun pointed at them. I need to buy some more time. "Where are you, Tony?" I don't hear a response. I look at Zack. "Why did you host such an elaborate trap then? Why place the prisoners where we can easily find them?"

Zack looks more than happy that I asked this question; he is overjoyed. "Ah, Willow. You are quite smart. I always thought that you are possibly one of the only girls with a brain capability close to mine. Not quite as amazing as mine, but close..." He holds out his hands, "You see, when I injected your blood into me I only got the powers you had up until the point I took your blood. I want all of the powers, not just some..."

The realization hits hard and I raise my upper lip in disgust. "You wanted me to run into those people so I'd get their powers. Then you could take my blood and have all of them!" It comes out more of a question than a statement.

Zack starts clapping loudly. "Bravo, Willow, Bravo!"

"Then what did you inject Tony with? Why did you make him a Reaper?" I yell.

"I didn't make him a Reaper." Zack laughs.

Huh? "If you didn't inject him with something to turn him into a Reaper, then what did you do to him?"

He raises his lip in a half smile. "I need an army. He'll be one of my soldiers."

"No! He will not!" I yell. My fists are clenched and the anger is tearing at my vision until the edges blur with red. Or is it gold?

"Yes he will. Come on out, Tony," he calls behind him. I watch in horror as Tony steps out from behind a mirror upon command. His eyes are red and he complies.

"Tony, help me. You have to snap out of this," I beg him.

"No, sugar. He can't snap out of this... unless, of course, you want to give yourself up freely. Then maybe I can change him back," Tony says to me, but I know it's not Tony. It's really Zack.

"Let my friends go," I point to Candy, Alec, and Jake.

Zack looks at me like I'm crazy for wanting to help them. Then he shrugs and says, "Why not." He turns to the guys who I thought were Reapers. "Let them go."

I wait until they are gone and then I say, "You will have to kill me before I go anywhere with you." I smile snidely in the same way he has been doing to me. Then I raise my gun to my forehead.

The Reapers, or whatever they are, start advancing. "Stop!" Zack yells. He turns his glaring eyes at me. "Two can play at this game. Tony, shoot yourself."

My hand starts shaking as I see Tony slowly raise his gun up towards his own head.

"No!!!" "No!" I yell aloud and inside Tony's head. Then the anger that had been threatening overcomes me. The edges of my vision seem to fill with a golden haze. My arms shake and the gun falls from my hands. I clench my fists and the anger pours through my veins. I can feel it flooding over me.

The mirrors start bursting forth. The glass shatters everywhere like silver confetti. The lights overhead explode, sending down fireworks of red ember sparks. The ground shakes. An earthquake is tearing at the building but I don't care. I aim my anger at Zack. His eyes turn from shock to fear and he begins backing away. A beam from the ceiling lands behind him. I realize then that I caused it to fall. I'm causing this building to shake. I hold out my hands and watch as pieces of the ceiling break through and fall to the ground. They crush the mirrors behind Zack and block his escape route. More beams fall and the ground trembles. I realize in horror that I can't control whatever is happening. The ceiling starts caving in and I look up to find a beam hanging dangerously low above my head.

Suddenly, Tony snaps out of it. His eyes turn yellow and I look at him with some relief. "You have to stop, Willow!"

"I can't!" I realize that I have no control over this power I'm yielding.

Zack has backed up and is trying to get away through another corridor. I throw a beam in his way and he falls back on his butt.

Then the air is whooshed out of me as Tony grabs me over his shoulder so quickly that in the next second we are outside. We escape just in time; right before the entire ceiling comes crashing down.

ELEVEN

It takes me a moment before I catch my breath and my heartbeat returns to normal.

Tony holds onto me for a few seconds longer and then puts me down carefully. "Are you okay?" he asks me in our own internal language.

I look up at the neon yellow eyes of the man I can't help but find myself falling for. I nod my head. My body is still shaking and the gold is fading away from my field of sight. "Yes, thank you. I didn't think I could stop... It just kept coming down. I wanted it all to come down." I find myself frightened by the power of this new gift. I could have kept going and buried us all if Tony had not stepped in and saved me.

Tony sees the fear in my eyes. He lifts his hand to my cheek, "I will never let anything happen to you." My heart starts accelerating, but not because of fear this time. I lean my cheek further into his hand, accepting the warmth and security he provides me with.

Screams and shouts in the distance pull me from my stupor. I turn around and see just how far Tony had taken me from the ruined building. We are well over a hundred yards away, but I can still see all of my friends looking through the heaping remains. They haven't noticed Tony and me yet and they cry out my name over and over.

Realizing what they must be thinking, I dash towards them.

"No!" Alec yells as he digs in the pile of rubble. He begins pulling off brick after brick, digging… calling my name.

My heart drops and I sprint the last few yards to his side. "Alec, Alec, I'm right here!" I yell, feeling horrible that he thinks something bad has happened to me. It's not until I place my hands on his shoulders that he finally understands that I'm not buried in the pile of debris.

He pulls me into him tightly, holding onto me for dear life. I can hear his heart still beating fast from the adrenaline. "Willow, I was so scared," he says to me in a shaky whisper. I rub his back to comfort him, not caring that Tony is probably glaring behind me. A handful more seconds pass and he finally lets out a deep breath. He holds me at arm's length. "If anything were to happen to you…" He shakes his head in disbelief, not being able to finish the sentence.

Claire and Connor, who have been standing next to us, join in on the hug. The relief is apparent in their tear-filled eyes. We hold onto each other in one large bear hug on this tall pile of rubble.

"I told you to go to the perimeter. It wasn't safe here," I say to Claire and Connor.

"Yeah, we know what you told us but there was no

way we were leaving you three to deal with Zack alone," Connor states.

"We dropped the boy off and then we heard the screaming. Connor just pulled me through the maze walls. Then we saw Alec and Candy and the building falling in on itself." She hits me in the arm. "Don't ever do that to me again!" she yells at me while wiping the tears off her cheeks.

I rub my arm even though it didn't really hurt. "I certainly wasn't trying to do anything!" With her hand on her tiny hip and that mama bear expression of hers, I can't help but smile. "Okay, I promise that I will never do that to you again... intentionally." I have to add the last part because there's no way for me to truly promise that I won't run into danger in the future. I can't sit on the sidelines and let things happen; it's just not in my nature.

She raises one eyebrow and then pulls me into another quick hug. "Fair enough."

We both laugh at that. I look over Claire's shoulder and notice that Candy is sitting by herself, hugging her legs tightly to her chest. She looks small and scared. Jake is standing behind her looking like he wants to help her but he can't. She must have told him to leave her alone or something. I excuse myself from my friends.

I walk over to Candy and crouch down at her side. "Hey," I say simply.

Her head lifts up a few inches. She stares at the rubble behind me. Her blue eyes are rimmed with unshed tears. "Do you think he's dead?"

I look back at the mess that was once a building.

If he's not dead, then I have no idea how he would have gotten out. There doesn't seem to be a beam standing in the place. "I don't know. We can look if you'd like."

She shakes her head much to my relief. "No, we need to get these people out of here."

I nod my head, not really sure what to say. I can't imagine the internal struggle that declaration must cause her. I can only guess that part of her justification is that if she doesn't find him then at least she can hope that the last of her family isn't dead.

She forces herself to look away from the wreckage and into my eyes. "Hey..." she hesitates a few seconds. "Willow, I just want to tell you how sorry I am. I'm just... so sorry I didn't believe you. I really thought he had changed... that he hadn't fallen under our dad's spell." Her eyes are rimmed in red and I can tell it's tearing her up inside. Having not only lost her father but now losing her brother in a matter of days... even if he's still alive, he's lost to her.

I put my arm around her, comforting her. "He's your blood, Candy. You had every right to think the best of him. That's what families do," I say, trying to give her peace of mind. "No one will hold it against you or tell you, 'I told you so'."

She sniffles. "Thanks," she says simply. "I guess I just don't know what to do from here. I feel so isolated... like I've lost everything important to me. Who am I supposed to be if I'm all alone?"

I listen with an open heart. I can feel her loss and

pain. "You'll always have us," I tell her. "And no matter what, you will always be you. Family doesn't define who you are. They mold and shape you when you are young and pliable but eventually it is up to us all to define ourselves. You have already grown so much on your own without the help of your dad or brother. You'll continue along that path to become the amazing woman you are supposed to be. I believe in you, Candy." I watch her eyes light up a little. I don't know where those words came from. Part of me wants to think that my mother somehow spoke through me because it's definitely something she would say.

Candy gives me a small smile and nods in understanding. "You're right, I am amazing." I can't contain the laugh that comes from that. She laughs lightly in return before her expression turns somber again. She holds her hand over her heart and clenches the fabric of her shirt. "No, seriously. I don't know how I'm going to get through this. My heart is aching so badly that I wish I could just turn it off and not feel. I do know though, that you guys are here for me. I know I will make it past all of this pain. I just have to keep going."

I can understand the way she feels, so completely that it brings back the ache in my chest from my own loss. I nod my head, "Yes, just keep going. That's all any of us could expect or ask of you. It will get better. I'm not sure how soon, but it will." I help her to her feet and together we join the others. I smile as she allows Jake to pull her into his arms. I know he will be an integral part in this healing process.

Tony comes to my side and he and Alec share one of those macho handshakes. A smile flitters on my face, thankful they've put their differences and jealousy aside... at least for now.

"Alright," I say. "We still have a lot of work ahead of us. We need to go help find the others," I say, hoping there are other's to be saved.

We spend the next several hours walking the maze. We run into the other groups along the way who have found a few of the prisoners. When we find Mr. Leroy, he tells us that they've already found the group of prisoners that had been stashed in one of the buildings like John said. It seems like that is where most of them were hidden. We find nearly a hundred people in all. It's not as many as we had hoped for, but it's better than none. I groan in frustration as I realize there are more out there somewhere. In our best estimate, we believe that at least fifty more people from the shelter are still missing.

We don't have any luck finding Alec's dad. On the flip side, we do find Connor's parents. It is quite surprising that they are here since they weren't in the shelter or with my mom's people. I wouldn't have guessed that they would have been on the mountainside that day since they weren't accepted into the shelter to begin with. I put the idea aside for now.

Their neon yellow eyes are bright and tearful as they cling to Connor. He assures them that Lily is safe and sound. Their reunion is a tearful one. I'll admit I let more than one tear fall watching them together.

We find out that Connor's parents had been keeping a close eye on the shelter and when they saw the attack, they ran out in hopes of saving Connor and Lily. Before that, they had been hiding out in the cellar of a house not far from there. Apparently, the previous owners of the home, who we assume had been accepted into the shelter, had stocked it with several months of rations and everything they needed to survive. I had heard about dooms day shelters in the past, I just didn't know any still existed. We allow them a few minutes to reconnect before we get moving again.

We make it out of the Maze Ruins without losing anyone. We convene with everyone else and do a quick debriefing before we head back to the safe house. We arrive back late at night. As always, the adults have held off on dinner until our return. They come piling out when our mighty big group walks up. It's a happy reunion, full of joy. We lost no one and brought back nearly a hundred more. I can't help but smile as many families are reunited.

As tradition goes, after dinner someone starts a bonfire and pulls out the S'mores. The music begins playing and we take the time to forget all of our hardship and just have fun. I find my dad and Sabby in the throng of people. They are standing in line to get marshmallows. "Hey there guys," I call to them.

My dad turns around and smiles at me. "Hey honey," he says.

"Look, Wello!" Sabby turns to me with his skewer filled to the brim with four large marshmallows.

"Wow, Sabby!" I point to the girl standing at the table handing out the sugary treats. "That girl over there must have thought you were the most handsome man here to have given you that many marshmallows," I kid with him.

He shrugs his shoulders and grins. "I am hansome, Wello!"

We all giggle. My dad turns his attention to me and repeats what he's been saying repeatedly since I returned. "I'm so proud of you, Willow."

"Ize proud of you too!" Sabby hugs my leg and nearly pokes my dad in the stomach with his marshmallow skewer.

"Thanks guys." I smile. Looking at my dad and my baby brother, something tells me that things may turn out okay after all. I still have family left on this Earth and I plan on making the most of this life I've been blessed with. I plan to make my mother proud.

We laugh as we toast marshmallows and listen to Sabby tell us a new joke he learned today that makes absolutely no sense. The smiles and laughter aren't exactly what they'd been in the past, but they are a start towards the long journey of healing.

Alec comes to my side and asks me for a dance. I accept and allow him to pull me out to the dance floor.

"Are we okay?" Alec asks me.

I look up at him. "Yes, why do you ask?"

He shakes his head. "I just want to make sure. Today has really left me thinking. I can't imagine my life without you in it." My mouth drops slightly and I get ready to say something but he continues before I can. "I just want to be in it, Willow. If that's as your friend, we will have to make it work."

"I know," I tell him. "We will." I smile up at him.

His face turns serious as he asks me, "Are you falling for him?"

I look up at him like a deer caught in headlights. "I..."

He holds his hand out. "Wait, don't answer that. Not yet at least. I'm sorry I asked."

I sigh and lean my forehead against his chest. "Okay," I say, not sure where to go from here. I can feel it in every ounce of my being what Alec wanted me to say. He wanted me to tell him no, I'm not falling for Tony, but that would have been a lie.

We finish dancing to the song in silence and then Claire pulls me away from Alec. "My turn!" she says mischievously.

I mouth, "thank you," to Claire. A fast song is playing and we dance to it. Candy walks by and Claire pulls her into our circle. We laugh and twirl around to a few more songs while singing the ones we know. We kick off our shoes and dance barefoot after a while. For those few songs, we pretend like life isn't the crazy tilt-o-whirl that it's become. We pretend that we are just teenage girls who haven't a care in the world.

When a slow song begins to play, I step away to catch my breath. I push my sweaty hair from out of my eyes and lean up against the courtyard wall.

A few seconds later, Tony is at my side. "May I have this dance?" he asks, holding out his hand. I give him an embarrassed smile, what with him catching me completely off guard. I hadn't seen him all night. I put my hand in his and he leads me to the center of the party where other couples have gathered to dance.

I spy Connor and Claire a few yards away, dancing and gazing in each other's eyes sweetly. Tony twirls me around, then places one arm on the small of my back and the other in my hand. I rest my head on his shoulder and sway with the music. He twirls me a few times intermittently and I smile in delight.

"I'd say things went pretty well today, wouldn't you?" I ask Tony.

He gives me his manly half smile. "I'd say you're right."

I place my head back on his shoulder and let him lead me in the dance. My hand begins cramping and I try letting go but can't. I lift my head from his shoulder and look at him worriedly. "Tony, can you let my hand go? It's starting to hurt." He's squeezing it tightly.

He's looking away. From this point of view, I can see that his gaze is distant, focused on nothing in particular. "Tony," I say a little more forcefully, while trying to jerk my hand away.

He finally looks back at me, red eyes in tow. I suck in a breath, being taken completely off guard. I panic, not wanting everyone around me to know what's happening.

Before I can begin healing him, he speaks. "You think you've won now… I've only just begun. Your precious Tony is about to become my little puppet. I'd take this time to say goodbye if I were you, because there's nothing you can do about this, sugar."

I involuntarily shutter at Zack's pet name for me. I don't waste any more time before I go into full-blown healing mode. I heal like I've never healed before. The only other time I let myself go this far was when I healed my mom at the side of the mountain.

A few minutes pass before I finally feel my hand release from his grip. I look up at Tony with droopy eyes. He looks confused. He must not remember any of these episodes.

"Sorry, I'm tired all the sudden. Do you mind walking me back to my room?" I ask. His confusion doesn't waver but he agrees. I say goodbye to my friends, who happen to be in the path between where I was standing and the door. I'm so weak my legs can barely carry me.

TWELVE

I wake in the middle of the night not quite sure how I got to my bed. I sit up rubbing my eyes.

Thoughts from last night haunt my memory. "Tony," I say instinctively. I can feel it deep down inside me that his days are numbered. If only I knew exactly how many days I had left with him… or could it be just hours? The gift I have of seeing a short distance into the future isn't very helpful with that. Especially since the visions only come here and there. Unlike the other powers, I haven't been able to find a way to control that one.

I don't need to see the future though to know I need to get Tony out of here. I wish I could say that we need to leave so that these last few days can be ones of peace and tranquility for him. But the truth of the matter is, I have to get him away from all of these innocent people. I am now one of their leaders and I can't allow anything to happen to them.

I get out a pencil and paper from the nightstand next to me and write a note.

Dear Dad,
I'm going somewhere for a few days. Please don't worry; I'll be
okay. There are just a few things I need to take care of. Give
Sabby a hug for me and I'll see you soon.
Love Always,
Willow

It's not much, but I hope it'll help him not to worry while I'm gone. I gather up a few essential items from my room and cram them into a backpack. I change into a pair of cut-off shorts and a white shirt and then head out. I get out to the hallway and realize I don't know where Tony's room is. I grit my teeth in frustration. I have all these gifts at my disposal but I can't find someone's room. It seems ridiculous. I'm pretty sure he's in this hallway, but this is a huge building. In reality, he could be anywhere!

"Where do you think you're going?" someone questions behind me. I turn around, startled. One of the older women, who I think must mistake me for a younger kid, stares me down with a questioning look.

"Umm," I stammer, trying to figure out what to say to her. Then, against my better judgment, I use my compulsion. "Tell me where Tony's room is." As always, her eyes glaze over and she goes into robot mode.

"Tony who?" she asks. I didn't realize someone could ask a question under compulsion. I guess if they don't know the answer to something they can. I'll play around with that later.

"Tony, the one who is my second in command."

She looks at me as if just now realizing who I am. Then she immediately answers. "Floor three, room 315."

I thank her and ask another question. "Why do our noses run and our feet smell?"

Her expression is priceless. She just gives me a blank stare; my guess is that she's searching the far recesses of her brain to come up with an answer. "I. Don't. Know," she says awkwardly.

"Thank you for your help," I tell her before I take off for the stairs. I'm on floor two so Tony's just one floor above me. It only takes me a few moments to find his room but when I get there, I just stop and stare at the door. What if he's not dressed? What if he's not alone…? I push the goofy thoughts aside and knock softly. When he doesn't answer, I gather enough guts to enter. I find it locked so I move through the door.

His room is illuminated by the soft light of the moon and stars that trickles in through the open window. Tony's fast asleep, wearing his pajama bottoms… and no shirt. I can feel my face go red. It just feels wrong watching him sleeping, so intimate.

I swallow the lump in my throat and give him a light shake. "Tony," I whisper.

He doesn't respond so I repeat my actions. The third time, I really shake him and his eyes flutter open. Once he realizes it's me, he bolts upright throwing me off-guard. "Willow, what's wrong? Is everything okay?"

I nod my head. "Yeah, everything's fine. I just…" Sheeze. How do I ask him this? "I just wanted to see if you'll do me a favor."

He rubs his eyes, looking slightly confused. My eyes wander in his silence. I try not looking at his perfectly sculpted chest but I find myself losing the battle. He's just so… utterly beautiful. He raises his eyebrows at me and I purse my lips.

"Like what you see?" he asks me playfully.

I turn a hundred shades of red and look away. "Yes," I say bashfully. "I'll just wait outside the door."

A minute or so goes by before he quietly opens the door and meets me in the hall. Thankfully, this time, he's wearing a shirt. Now at least I'll be able to look him in the eyes without being distracted.

"You know how you said back at the cabin that you'd do anything for me?"

He gives me a look that says 'Oh boy, what have I gotten myself into.' "MmHm," he mutters.

"Well, I want you to take me somewhere; away from here."

I guess he realizes it isn't as bad as he thought. He gives me a slight head nod. "And, how long is this little excursion going to be?"

I shrug my shoulders. "I don't know, a few days? We'd have to leave now though," I say, hoping he'll say yes.

He stares at me for quite a long time, but I don't dare look away. Finally, he agrees. "Let me just get a few things together. I'll meet you at your room in ten."

I'm surprised he's not asking more questions. Grateful, I nod my head and walk back to my room to wait.

When I get back to my room, I find the note my mother wrote me in the back pocket of my old jeans. I can't believe I almost forgot it! I've decided that I'm going to open it with Tony. Maybe tomorrow. It seems like every time I think about opening it, I chicken out. It just seems so final to me. Like her death is a done deal. It's with this letter that I hold onto the last bit of her that's still alive in my heart. I squeeze the note in my hand. "I love you, Mom," I say , hoping that she can still hear me. I stick the letter into the back pocket of my jean shorts.

A knock raps on the door and I get up and answer it. Tony stands at the door leaning against the frame. "So, where to?" he asks. He's dressed in jeans that fall low on the hips and a white shirt. Yum.

"I want to go back to your place," I answer nervously. As soon as I say it out loud, I realize how that sounded. Tony stifles a laugh as I rush to explain myself. "No! That's totally not what I meant!"

He can't suppress the laugh anymore. So he doesn't wake up the entire hall he lets himself in my room and shuts the door. "So, you want to go back to my place, yet we haven't actually defined our relationship."

I punch him playfully in the chest. "You know that's not what I meant!" He grins and I bite my lip. "Well… that's the one place where we can forget all of this," I say, gesturing to our surroundings with my hand. "I just need to get away for a while is all."

He seems to ponder what I said for a second, and then he agrees. "Did you let your dad know?"

I show him the note. "Alright then. Your wish is my command," he says. I smile brightly, and then pick up my backpack off the floor. "But, no funny business," Tony adds playfully.

I stifle a laugh and off we go.

We decide to run for it. Tony holds my hand as we run and he helps me dodge the trees. It's crazy how good his reflexes are. When I duck under a fallen branch, I realize mine aren't too shabby either.

We get to Tony's cabin right before dawn. He makes us some hot tea and we sit out on the porch swing with a thick quilt and watch the sun rise. Tony wraps his arm around me and I can't help but feel unbelievably safe in his embrace. I nestle into him and sip the hot tea.

Tony kisses me on the top of my head. "We have some unfinished business to take care of."

I get goose bumps along my arms. "We do?" I ask, lost. A thousand things roll through my mind.

"MmHm," he murmurs. "Our earlier conversation brought something to light. We haven't defined our relationship. And… I don't know about you, but I'm eager to do so."

My stomach erupts in butterflies. I really like Tony. Like, really like him. But, I know what's about to happen to him. And I don't know if I can handle losing somebody else right now. On the flip side, I've vowed to make these last, however many, days some of his best. If that includes letting him call me his girlfriend, then so be it. I lift my head upwards to face him.

He gazes down at me and gives me a smile that warms my blood and melts my heart. "Willow Mosby, will you do the honor of being my girlfriend?"

It's either the way he phrases it so simply or the fact that he's so cute, that causes me to giggle.

"What?" He pokes me in the ribs, causing me to squirm.

"Watch it!" I giggle, trying not to spill my tea. I reach down, setting it on the ground.

Tony sits up, letting his yellow eyes rest on mine. He takes my hands in his and I savor the warmth that flows from him into me. "I'm being serious, Willow. There was... is something about you that makes me want to be a better man. I was honored when your mother asked me to be your protector and I took my job seriously. Still do! It's just—I've always wanted something more. I wanted the right to hold your hand in public, for everyone to know that you were mine and I was yours. Maybe it sounds cheesy, but I'd love to be your boyfriend. I promise I'd treat you right and always keep you safe. I'll never mistreat you or give you any less than you deserve. You just don't know how long I've waited for someone like you."

My breath catches, realizing his profession of love for me. He may not have said those three words, but I can feel it on his mind. My heart aches knowing what is to come. I push the thoughts of his imminent future aside and figure to live in the now. I remember the quote my mother liked to tell me. 'It's better to have loved and lost than never to have loved at all.' I smile up at Tony and squeeze his hand. "I'd be honored," I answer with a sincere smile.

I can see the visible relief in his expression at my answer. He smiles and pushes the hair out of my eyes. He closes his eyes and leans in to kiss me. I close my eyes and then... I'm running! I'm taken to the night where I'm running down the dark street. Buildings blur as I run so fast that my heart is beating uncontrollably fast. He's not far behind me now and I know it's only a matter of time before I reach the point where I turn down the dead end alley. I can hear his shoes pounding against the pavement only a few feet from me. Something hot hits my legs and I feel the burn seeping across my skin.

He calls to me hauntingly just like before, "Willow!" I don't look back; I keep running. I've had this vision before. I know what happens; he will catch me. I don't know what happens after that, but it's inevitable. The ground starts shaking and I feel my body moving uncontrollably back and forth. "Willow!" My legs are burnt and the shaking makes it worse, but I feel my healing working. "Willow!"

Like a flash, I'm out of the night, out of the vision. I open my eyes to the light.

Tony stops shaking me. He stares at me with a look of concern and fear in his eyes. "What happened? What did you see?"

I look at him, taken aback. I'm still a little disoriented.

"Your eyes are copper, what did you see?" he asks me. I can't bring myself to answer him. He looks down at my legs, "Crap!" He jumps up from the swing and runs inside. In less than five seconds, he's back at my side with a damp cloth.

I look down before he places it on my leg. I must have dropped my cup of hot tea. The teacup is shattered on the ground at my feet and my leg is red and swelling from where the scolding hot water hit it.

Tony places the cloth on my skin and I grimace at the pain. I can feel myself healing, but it's slow. The thing I hate most about burns are that it's not a singular pain, it's like your skin keeps burning after the fact. I imagine in all actuality it kind of does. I close my eyes and focus on healing to help speed up the process and usher the pain away. A minute or two later, I open my eyes and look at Tony with relief. "Thanks."

Tony still looks concerned. "What did you see? By the way your entire pallor went ghost white, I can only assume it wasn't good."

I can't tell him what I saw without revealing the truth. How do I? Can I take this little bit of time away from him?

"You need to be honest with me, Willow," he tells me in the way only the two of us can communicate.

"I can't." How would I tell him something like this? I look away from his demanding eyes.

He reaches up, places his hand under my chin, and guides my gaze back to his. "You need to tell me." I plead with him using my eyes but he doesn't waver. "I deserve to know what the truth is. You can't hold back on me."

I know he's right. Would I want to know ahead of time what's about to happen? I can only imagine that I would. I close my eyes for a second to muster up the courage. He drops his hand, knowing that I'm about to relent. I open my eyes and take a deep breath. "I was in the room before you awoke back at the prison." I don't know exactly where to start, except for the beginning.

He looks at me in confusion so I continue. "I watched Zack inject you with something before you woke up. I would have stopped him but I couldn't. I didn't want to lose the chance of getting you free and I... I should have stopped him. I didn't know at first what it was or that it was you behind the curtain... Either way, I should have saved you!" Tears blur my vision. I know what I'm saying makes no sense, but I don't know how to tell him this.

Tony's hands go up to my shoulders and he looks at me strongly. "What do you mean, Willow? What did he inject me with?"

I shake my head, my words are lost, and the tears fall down my cheeks. A few land on my bare legs.

"Look, no matter what it's not your fault. You couldn't have taken Zack on, not with that army backing him. But you need to tell me, what did he inject me with?"

"The red shot," I barely manage to tell him with my mind.

At first he looks confused, then his look turns to pure horror. He jumps out of the porch swing so quickly that it sends it and me rocking fast. He runs his hands through his copper hair and pulls at the ends. He takes a few steps and whispers, "No..."

I jump out of the swing and put my hand on his back. I can't imagine what he's feeling. "I shouldn't have told you. I'm so sorry."

He turns on me so quickly that I nearly fall back. I right myself and accept the stare down that he's aiming my way. "How could you keep this from me?" His voice is filled with so much hurt that I don't know what to say.

I shake my head and stammer, "I... I don't know. I thought it was best. I thought I could heal you. I tried so many times..."

His eyes harden. "What do you mean, you tried so many times?"

I cringe and step back. My stomach feels like lead. I'm filled with so much dread that I can barely stand underneath its weight. "There have been some incidents. But, I was able to heal you and it was okay. You came back to me."

He looks horrified and disgusted. "There were incidents?" He runs his hand through his hair again and doubles over, looking at the ground. I can't imagine the inner turmoil he's struggling with right now. He stands back up and looks at me. "What kind of incidents? Did I hurt you?"

I can't go over them. No, he would surely send me away or he would leave me himself. He needs these last few days of humanity... I need these last few days with him. I shake my head. "It was okay. You were okay after I healed you. Please don't hate me. I just wanted to see if I could help you. Even though I haven't been able to stop it, I wanted you to have these last days. I didn't want you to be like this, to know what would eventually happen. It's not fair." I wipe away at the tears.

He looks away from me. I feel then that he will just walk away. He will leave me standing in the dust. I didn't tell him something he had every right to know. I kept it from him, even if I thought I was doing the right thing. He turns back and looks at me with his bright yellow eyes. The only eye color I want to remember him having. "I need to leave. I need to get you back to the safe house and leave." Realization creeps across his expression with those words. "Is that why you wanted me to come here with you?"

I stare at him, not knowing how to answer that question. I feel like someone has pulled the foundation away from my house of cards and they are toppling inward, slowly onto me. "I wanted to have these last few days with you." Be honest, Willow, I tell myself. "And I wanted to protect the others in case... or when the time comes for the change to take its full effect."

Tony's expression is so conflicted and wounded that it breaks me. I feel like I've caused this even though in all actuality Zack caused these events to be set in motion. I've only been treading water trying to stay afloat in the aftermath. Tony doesn't say anything more. He turns from me and walks away. He leaves me standing on his porch as I watch him disappear into the woods.

THIRTEEN

I am not sure if Tony will return.

I wait though. I don't leave the porch. Not when the sun meets the highest point in the sky and not when it begins its decent over the horizon. I sit on the porch swing, staring off at the lake and the mountains in the distance. The water looks ablaze with the yellows and oranges reflecting wildly against its surface. The mountains have the smallest peaks of white at their tips. The weather has turned cooler and the fact that snow has hit their tops, tells me that we may see a change in seasons coming soon, despite Project ELE.

I hug my legs into my body, trying to make myself smaller. My insides feel broken. I realize Tony isn't coming back. I don't know if I would either, if the roles were reversed. My foot has fallen asleep so I shuffle to a new position on the porch swing. The sound of rustling paper calls my attention. I reach into my back pocket and pull out the envelope with my mother's letter in it. It's crinkled and worn from my travels over the past few days.

I wish you were here, Mom. I don't stop the tear from falling down my cheek. I know it's probably a mind trick but I feel the paper warm in my hands as if my mother is telling me, "I am here, honey."

I look around. The wind rustles the leaves on the trees and somewhere in the distance I can hear the sound of birds chirping. I look back down at the letter in my hand. I close my eyes and try to feel my mom's spirit, her presence. I need her. I open my eyes and slowly work on the seal of the envelope with my fingers. When I've opened it, I pull out the sheets of paper. Time stops the moment I unfold it. All noise is silenced, and the world around me pauses, as I read my mother's final words to me.

My Dearest Willow,

If you are reading this, then I am gone. I didn't mean to leave you, my love, but I had no choice. Your life is far more valuable than mine. I don't know if you will ever truly understand that conviction until you lay eyes on your first child. Then it will click. You will fully understand why I did all that I've done. Until then, I can only attempt to explain my choice.

When your father told me his vision, I knew I couldn't allow it to happen. I would lay my life down a million times before I would allow any of my children to die. You know very well from the testing back before the shelter, that I could never stand to outlive any of my children. You see, my dearest Willow, if I hadn't sacrificed my life, your father's vision would have become a reality.

He had seen us standing outside of prison walls, surrounded by a crowd of people we've never seen before. Dr. Hastings and his son were trying to get you to reveal yourself by using us as

bait

I know you love us and there has never been any doubt of that love. If there had ever been an inkling, it would have been wiped away with that vision. I know how completely that love flows from you because of what your father saw. I only tell you this next part because I feel as if you need to fully understand all of the circumstances.

You accepted the bait and came forward. In that instant, Tony dashed out before you and shot Dr. Hastings dead. Another soldier shot Tony from behind. Your father told me how bravely you turned and lifted the pistol in your hands to take out the soldier behind you, but it wasn't quick enough. He shot you point blank in the forehead before you could pull the trigger.

Your father watched you die in that vision. I've never seen your father lose it like that before. I didn't think he would ever be right again. He could barely breathe; barely function with the knowledge of the future. After he told me the truth of what he saw, I felt the same way. That is why we both wrote you a letter. We did not know who would have the opportunity to save your life and give their life in return for so great a cause. I gave your father this letter and if you are reading this today, I am probably buried with the letter he wrote.

I don't know how I died, nor is that the point. I want you to know though, that there was a purpose in my death. That purpose is you. I've always known that you will accomplish great things, my child. I have no doubt that nothing will hold you back, not even the loss of your mother. I urge you to find a way to let me go, to know that I am in a better place. I want you to have the life your father and I have always dreamt of you having. A life after the virus, after these wars. A life that is filled with love and hope.

Willow, I know that you will find these things. You have already grown into a young woman whom I am so proud to call my daughter. You are strong, you are loving, and you are loyal, beautiful, caring and smart. You are going to make a great leader in my absence. Please don't freak out, but I told Mr. Leroy a while ago that you are the one who should take my place if anything were to happen to me. I don't know if he will accept my recommendation, but I know in my heart he would be stupid not to. If you are asked, be courageous, as I know you will be. You may think you are too young, too inexperienced, too weak, but you are none of those things. You are my daughter and age and experience are nothing except something you will grow into. You will be a fine leader; I have no doubt of that.

I love you so very much, my darling. When you miss me, look to the sky and know that I am watching you and that I love you and that I am so very proud of you. Please take care of your father and take care of Sebastian. He looks up to you so much and he is blessed to have such a great sister in you.

I love you with all of my heart and soul forever and ever. Death cannot take that away. Don't ever give up and always love, no matter what.

Love,
Mom

I stare at the last two words for what seems like hours. The sun has gone and the stars have taken its place.

Love,

Mom

My tears fall onto the paper, marking it with dark, wet circles. I can't bring myself to look away from the paper even though I can barely see it now in the moonlight. My mom gave her life for me. She knew it was going to happen in advance. She knew that either she or my dad would be taking my place.

My heart feels exposed and my chest feels heavy. I had not known how to completely process the fact that my mom had injected herself with that poison. I always wondered, what if... What if she had just waited? Maybe I could have saved her. What if I stepped forward and just gave them what they wanted, would she have survived?

Those questions are laid to rest with the words in this letter. My mom gave her life for me because if she had not, I would be gone. I look at the words, my mother's handwriting. I pull the letter against my chest and that's when it happens. I break down so completely that I crumple into the porch swing. I cry so hard that my sobs make it sway. The tears flow so freely that with every breath I feel as if a thousand weights are laid against my chest.

"Willow!" I hear my name called from afar.

Then a moment later, I'm pulled from the swing and I'm curled in his arms. He holds me tightly against him while he moves to sit with me in his lap. My mother's letter is crumpled between us. I duck my head into his chest and allow myself to lose it, to let it all out. He rubs my back and holds me securely against him. We stay like that for I don't know how long.

When the tears stop, I sit up and look at Tony. In his eyes, I see how he feels. I know that I have his heart; he's given it to me for safekeeping. I think perhaps, he may have mine too.

He pulls me into a hug and then he helps me to my feet. Without a word, he grabs my hand and takes me into the cabin.

He has me sit on the couch. Then, he lights a few lamps and begins working on making me something to eat. When he returns a little while later, he has two bowls of hot Ramen in his hands. He hands me one and then takes a seat next to me.

We eat in silence. After we finish, he puts the dishes away and lights a fire. We don't say anything to each other that night. He knows I read my mom's letter. He doesn't ask me what it said. I know he must still be hurt that I kept the facts about the shot away from him, but I don't ask him how he feels. I lie on the couch in his arms and watch the flames of the fire devour the wood until eventually my eyelids become heavy and I fall asleep.

FOURTEEN

I awake sometime after the sun has risen.

The embers are still glowing in the fireplace. Tony is already awake and making something that smells wonderful. I sit up and brush at my wild curls. My mother's letter is sitting on the floor beside the sofa. I gently pick it up and fold it neatly, then stick it back in my pocket.

"Good morning," Tony calls to me from the kitchen.

I stand up and walk over to him. He's changed into a tank top and sport shorts. He hands me a cup of tea. "Morning," I say groggily. My eyes feel heavy from all of the crying yesterday.

We sit down and eat a quiet breakfast made up of corn beef hash and canned potatoes. I've never had it before and while it looks unappetizingly disgusting, it tastes wonderful.

"Would you like to go for a walk?" Tony asks me.

I nod my head. "Yes, I'd like that very much." I'm still not sure where we stand. I know yesterday that he wanted me to be his girlfriend but did the fact that I kept the truth from him change the way he feels?

We clean up our breakfast dishes, and then we leave

the cabin. We walk down the steps and towards the lake. The sun is making its way above the mountain peaks to the east of the lake.

We don't talk but Tony does grab my hand. He squeezes it softly and leads me to the edge of the water. We walk around, along the shore for a ways. I watch the ripples of the water. Every once in a while a bird will fly low enough to touch the waves or a fish will jump into the air.

We make our way around a small bend on the shore. The grass had grown so high that I had not seen the small canoe that it hides. I look at it and then up to Tony.

"Okay, well maybe not so much as a walk than a sail," he says, breaking the silence. He tries to smile but it's hard for him to do. "Are you scared of the water?"

I shake my head. "No, I love the water." I have only been on a canoe once. It was before Sabby was born and when I was much younger. My parents took me out on a river during our summer vacation. I remember watching the Daddy-Long-Legs climbing all over the trees that lined the riverbanks. We had stopped to fish and I caught my first small trout. My mom and dad had made such a huge deal of it. They took a thousand pictures and I got mad because I wanted them to hurry so I could put the fish back where it belonged, in the water.

"Good." Tony pulls the canoe out of the tall grass without difficulty and flips it over on his own. He opens up his bag, pulls out a towel, and begins wiping out the inside of the boat. No doubt a legion of spiders are being removed from the home they've made theirs over these past several months.

I find two small oars in the grass next to where the boat was stored. I grab them as Tony starts to push the canoe into the water. He stops it halfway. "After you." He holds out his hand for me. I place the oars in the boat and then accept his hand. He helps me step in. The boat rocks as I make my way slowly to the other end.

He pushes the boat into the water as far as he can, before he jumps in and takes a seat on the bench facing me. He grabs an oar and hands one to me. He takes the other one and works on pushing us away from the shore.

The wind whips at my hair as we glide across the lake's surface. I close my eyes and feel the cool breeze against my skin. The air smells crisp and clean. The sun works counteractively against the coolness that the water-chilled wind brings. I savor the mix of cool and warmth. I open my eyes to find Tony staring at me. The heat in his eyes tells me that he hasn't completely written me off yet.

"I'm so sorry, Tony," I whisper, breaking the silence we've done so well to maintain.

This time he closes his eyes. He opens them a second later. "I can understand why you didn't tell me. I can only imagine that had the roles been reversed, I would have done the same."

Relief floods through me. "Even still, I'm so very sorry. I'm sorry that I wasn't able to stop it and I'm sorry that I didn't tell you."

Tony shakes his head. "You couldn't have stopped it from happening, Willow. That was out of your control. Yes, you could have told me about it afterwards, but I know why you didn't. For what it's worth, I forgive you completely."

I let out an audible breath. "Thank you," I whisper.

He nods once and then we go back to paddling. We make our way to the middle of the lake. Once we are at the point in which the mountains cast their image over our boat and past us into the water, we put down our oars. Tony rocks the canoe slightly as he moves off the bench and sits on the bottom of the boat between our two seats. He pats the narrow space next to him.

Not sure if I will fit, but not caring anyway, I move off my bench and sit beside him. The space between the two seats is enough for us to lie down if we keep our knees bent. He lies down first and then I lie down and rest my head on his chest.

My arm rests on top of his. I can hear his heart beating in my ears. It sounds beautiful. I close my eyes and savor the memory. The way he smells of grass and soap, the way the air feels against our skin, the gentle swaying of the boat against the lake's water... everything.

We lay like that for a while. Eventually I turn so that I can watch the white puffs of cumulous clouds float across the sky. We take turns calling out shapes in the clouds that our imagination has conjured up. The clouds look like huge pillows of white that tower up into Heaven. I like to imagine that my mom is up there looking down at us. I wonder what she would think of me being here with Tony. Would she approve of my choice between the two guys?

"Willow..." Tony says softly to get my attention.

"Mmhm?" I answer lazily.

"What are you thinking?"

I turn my head up so I can see his yellow eyes and answer. "About my mom. I wonder if she can see me."

He gently brushes my hair back as he says, "I'm sure she can."

I smile lightly and turn my eyes back to the sky. "What are you thinking?" I ask him in return.

"About you," he says warmly.

My stomach flutters. I look back up at him and he continues. "Yesterday, I was going to leave. I did make it as far as the empty prison yard before I turned back. I knew that the best thing would be for me to get as far away from you as I could, that it was the right thing to do."

I look at him worriedly and hold my breath, not sure where he's going with this.

"But I am a selfish man, Willow. I couldn't leave. I know that it's safer for you if I did... leave. But, if I'm going to lose myself soon, I don't want to do it until I've found myself first." He runs his fingers across my hand. "I felt like a shell before I met you. I went through the motions, I did my duty to serve and protect, but I didn't know who I was. When I first saw you on that mountainside, something in me changed. Time stopped and at that moment, I was torn between my duty to protect your mother and my desire to help you. You looked so scared and lost."

I think back to that day that wasn't too long ago. "You were going to shoot me," I joke.

He shakes his head. "I don't know if I would have been able to. If any other set of eyes had looked up at me, I wouldn't have hesitated. I never hesitated, before I met you."

I stare into his eyes, not sure what to say to such an honest sentiment.

"Willow Mosby, when I look at you, all of the broken pieces fit back together. I know I should leave and never come back, but I can't without telling you how I really feel. I can't imagine ever losing touch with who I am so much so that I wouldn't recognize what you mean to me. I know they say that..." he swallows and looks away, "Reapers, aren't in touch with their humanity," he looks back at me, his eyes full with emotion. "But, I will never forget that I am so in love with you that sometimes it hurts."

My breath catches as I stare into his eyes.

"Even if I don't remember this tomorrow, I couldn't bring myself to leave without telling you how much you mean to me and how I really feel. I love you and I will never stop loving you no matter how I change or who I become." He sits up on his elbow so that he's leaning slightly over me.

I can see the clouds behind him floating in the distance like a beautiful backdrop to a perfect picture. I look into Tony's eyes, mesmerized by the warmth and love conveyed in those yellow irises. My eyes wander down to his lips.

Tony lifts his hand and gently grazes it across my cheek. I close my eyes, savoring in his touch and the warmth that the sunshine brings. When I open them again,

I see his eyes staring at my lips in return. His gaze is filled with heat that sends a warm tingling sensation through my veins. My stomach dances as he moves in and kisses my forehead gently. I take a deep breath and hold it, not sure if that is all he was moving in for. He then kisses the bridge of my nose.

He pauses and I open my eyes to meet his. He looks at me; his eyes are asking me if it's okay. "I love you," he whispers in my mind. He leans in, his eyes close and so do mine, and then, after what seems like an eternity of waiting, his lips touch mine. A spiraling sensation flutters throughout me as my blood pumps wildly. He kisses me gently and everything inside me tells me that this is right. How I feel can't be put into words. I wrap my hands around his neck and pull him closer to me. Our kiss grows stronger and I run my hands through his hair. Fireworks burst forth behind my eyes and my toes curl as I allow the love to flow through me.

I feel the boat sway as our lips part and he sits up slightly. I don't want to open my eyes. I want to savor in the warmth and the feeling of electricity that course through me and touches every nerve ending in my body. I smile and take a deep breath. Then I open my eyes groggily. I stare up at the man that I very well may be falling in love with.

Tony stares back at me with a smile across his lips. He gently brushes a loose strand of hair behind my ear and then his hand freezes. His posture stiffens and his back goes rigid. Then before my eyes, I watch the eclipse happen in slow motion. My heart jumps and the panic takes hold as

I look on with pure dread. Like storm clouds moving in to cover the sun, his eyes fade from the bright, beautiful yellow that I adore into a deep, crimson red. Without thinking, I place my hands on his chest and focus my healing energies on him, desperately trying to save him. Seconds turn to minutes. He hasn't moved. He just sits upright staring at me with those eerie red eyes that only moments ago held a profession of love.

I feel my body going weak as I exert all the power I can on healing Tony. This time seems different though. This time it doesn't seem to be working. A tear slips down my cheek as I realize this may be it. How can such a loving moment turn into terror so quickly? Saving the last drop of energy, I release my hand from his chest.

An elfish grin encompasses his face; an expression I've never seen him make. I move away from him and scoot back as far as I can until I hit the back of the boat. Tony's lips part, "It's my turn now, sugar."

EPILOGUE

My breath catches and, at first, I freeze like you do in those horrible nightmares.

My body feels paralyzed with fear. The man I'm falling for stares back at me with crimson eyes that don't belong to him.

I'm stuck in the middle of a freaking lake in the middle of nowhere. How could I have been so stupid? "Tony, please come back to me," I beg him. My heart accelerates and I work hard to keep the panic at bay.

He cocks his head to the side and gives me a surprised look. "Wow sugar, you do have some great new gifts for me don't you?" I give him my coldest glare when he smiles. He rubs his hands together as if he's about to have the best meal of his life. "Now I need to take you in." He grabs an oar and starts rowing the boat back towards the shore.

I sit there watching his arms move the paddle back and forth, back and forth. The mountains surrounding the lake once looked majestic, now they look like prison walls locking me in on all sides. I have to consider all of my options. I can either try to get away now or I can wait until we get to the shore. I glance down at the water rippling against the boat.

Tony stops rowing and looks at me seriously. "Don't think about jumping ship, Willow. There is nowhere for you to go out here."

I memorize the way that my Tony looks. His copper hair shines like a penny underneath the sunbeams. His lips still make my stomach flutter with anticipation. I try to look past the red irises and remember the bright yellow eyes that once looked at me so adoringly. I don't want to forget what he looks like. I want to remember the real Tony, no matter what happens next.

I reach my hand into my back pocket and feel the letter sitting there safely. I look up at the clouds, hoping that my mom is looking out for me. I can hear her speaking the words from her letter, "Don't ever give up..."

I close my eyes and stand. I know what I have to do. My hands are behind my back and in one of them I hold an oar. My legs are shaky but I manage to maintain my balance. I keep my eyes closed as I whisper, "Zack, have I ever told you that I can't swim?"

I don't reopen my eyes so I have no idea how he will react to my proclamation. He takes the bait since I will be no use to him if I drown. I feel the boat waver as he makes a move towards me. I lean to the left, pretending to lose my balance. He is in front of me in an instant, ready to keep me from falling.

Using all of my strength, I open my neon yellow eyes and swing the oar out from behind me. Before he can register what I am going to do next, I bash it across his back with all my might. I watch as he goes tumbling forward into the lake. Water splashes against me, soaking into my clothes. I shiver.

I struggle against the part of myself that wants to help Tony and make sure he doesn't drown. I can't allow that part to win. Instead, I focus my mind on getting to shore. As the gold starts outlining my vision with a shiny haze, the boat moves a fraction of an inch. I take several deep breaths trying to get my mind to work with this new power.

I nearly fall off my seat when Tony's hand reaches up out of the water and grabs the edge of the boat. I keep from crying out as my heart works double time. I have to get out of here! I raise my shaking hands over my ears trying to block out the threats Tony is calling out to me from in the water. He tries to shake the boat more. To knock me out of it or to get into it, I'm not really sure.

The gold haze starts moving in again and, with much relief, the canoe starts propelling itself across the water with the speed of an Olympic rowboat. I turn and see Tony starting to swim after me. I leave him far behind in the wake, even with his strength and speed, he's no match for this boat. In less than two minutes, the boat hits the shore. I jump out of it and run. I run into the shadows of the forest. Tree limbs slap against my skin, causing lacerations that I will heal later. I jump over exposed roots and fallen limbs.

I don't look back because if I do, I know that I

might hesitate. I might go back to see if there is any way I can reach the Tony that I know is still inside there. I can't risk that, not now. If it were just my life in danger, my decision may have been different. Now, I am responsible for many others. I must get back to the safe house to warn everyone that they need to leave. Tony knows its location; it will only be a matter of time before Zack and his minions surround us. I have to save my people.

Then, after everyone is safe, I will go back for Tony. If there is no way to fix him, I know I will be forced to make a choice nobody should have to make. Allow him to keep hunting me forever, or kill him. The thought sends dread coursing through my body.

No! Until that decision must be made, I will not stop looking for a cure. I have to find a way to change Tony back. There has to be some way... This can't be final. I won't let Zack win. I will not lose Tony!

My mom's last few words come to mind, as I run through the trees. "...And always love no matter what."

To Be Continued...

EYE COLOR LIST

Eye colors and the abilities they correlate to:

Dark Green- Ability to read minds and hear thoughts. (Willow's first gift. Willow's original eye color: brown. Willow also absorbs other people's gifts when she is around them for a certain period of time. They still don't know how this is possible but some believe it's because she has a bit of Reaper in her. However, there is one major difference between Willow and a Reaper: Willow is still in touch with her humanity.)

Dark Blue- Ability to heal. (Alec's gift. Alec's original eye color: Emerald Green)

Hazel-yellow/green- Ability to compel people and make them do or believe what you tell them. (Zack's gift. Zack's original eye color: light brown)

Purple- Ability to turn invisible (Claire's gift. Claire's original eye color: icy blue)

Brown- Ability to change molecular structure and walk or pass through objects. (Connor's gift. Connor's original eye color- black)

Light Blue- Ability to see through people's abilities

or see when someone is using a gift. (Candy's gift. Candy's original eye color: light brown)

Neon Yellow- Ability to possess great strength, speed, agility and immunity. Rarely, if ever, does someone with this ability get sick. (Willow's mom, whose name is Alice, Sebastian and Tony's gift. As well as everyone else in the first compound. Alice and Sebastian's original eye color: Baby Blue. Tony's original eye color: Hazel Green.

Copper Orange- Ability to see visions of the near future. This is an ability that is new to everyone. Nobody knows how far in the future this ability will allow it's posseser to see, but currently Willow's dad has only been able to see a few minutes and no more than an hour ahead of time. In addition, with the knowledge of what lies ahead, they have been able to change the future outcome. For example, Willow didn't die during the attack on the hotel like the dad foresaw. (Willow's dad: Henry's gift.)

Black- Ability to read other people's emotions and intentions. In addition this ability allows the possessor to control the emotions of others. (Erik's gift.)

Red- Reapers, steal other people's abilities and drain their life from them. Not a lot is known about this power. Some believe that once a Reaper takes from someone that they only possess the ability for a limited period of time. This requires them to continually search for abilities to consume or in other words to help them power up. Because the process of reaping takes a lot of energy and a few minutes to completely drain a person, they don't bother using their powers on the people with yellow eyes.

After all, the Reapers currently possess this ability since it was their first gift before they took the red shot that was supposed to cause instant death. Instead that shot caused the death of their humanity.

Gold- Telekinesis. Ability to move objects with one's mind. (Marya and John's gift.)

Grey/Silver- A gift we know little about. All we know is that the one person Willow has met with this eye color was not susceptible to Willow's other powers. In fact, she had to truly trust the person in order to allow a gift to work. (Jennifer's gift.)

ACKNOWLEDGEMENTS

Wow, God has blessed us to be able to do something that before had only been a pipe dream. We had no idea when we started on this adventure that we would finish one book, let alone four books. We are extremely grateful for the success he has granted us and for his biggest blessing of all, our Lord Jesus. (Philippians 4:13)

We appreciate all of the support we have received from book blogs, our favorite Facebook pages, our family and friends and most of all from our fans. Your encouragement keeps us writing. All of your Facebook posts, Goodreads comments and emails that told us that you loved our books; it makes our hearts soar and makes us want to write even better for you. Thank you to everyone who has taken the time to review our book and thank you to everyone who continues to read our work. A shout out to Cynthia Shepp our editor, for making Exposing ELE shine.

To Marya Heiman with Strong Image Editing: Can we just say that you totally rock our socks?! No words can express how much we appreciate and value the beautiful covers that you have created for each of our books. Your covers are the icing to our cake. If the icing didn't look beautiful or taste delightful, nobody would try the cake. You make our book look yummy to the tummy! <3

To our friends who support our writing and allow us to talk for endless hours about our books at girl's nights, we are forever grateful: Dyan Brown, Marya Heiman, Kat Simon and Carol Cook.

Last but not least: a giant thank you to our Awesome Sauce Street Team who are out there on the front lines helping us spread the word about our books. We love you all! Mega love goes out to the most active members of our team: Alicia Guest Hall, Amy Stogner, Belinda Gallant, Brittany Willis, Cassie Chavez, Cassie Hoffman, Colleen Reilly, Cynthia Shepp, Heather Heslip Alexander, Heather Piantanida-pipes, Irayda Quezada, Jaime Cross, Jaime Radalyac, Jovhanna Caltzontzi, Karissa Stephens, Kathleen Guardado, Kristin Scearce Kim, Kristy Hamilton, Krystal Marlein, Lauren Dootson, Lela Lawing, Lisa Sasso, Lori Decker Fenn, Mayra Arellano, Melanie Martin, Melanie Newton, Michele Skinner, Natalie Walker Idrogo, Nikki Archer, Pam Mandigo, Samantha Truesdale, Tonya Carter Bunch.

ABOUT THE AUTHORS

      Rebecca and Courtney are downhome country girls powered by chocolate and other random late night cravings. Coined in southern twang they bring new meaning to the word y'all. BFI's since the 6th grade, with a knack for getting into sticky situations, has resulted in countless ideas to write about for years to come.

CONNECT WITH US

We would love to hear from you! Please come visit us:

Facebook:
http://www.facebook.com/eleseries

Twitter:
Courtney: http://www.twitter.com/nuckelsc
Rebecca: http://www.twitter.com/midnitebeckie

Webpage:

http://www.eleseries.com

CPSIA information can be obtained
at www.ICGtesting.com
Printed in the USA
LVOW03s0914070717
540549LV00001B/30/P